Goodrich Samuel Griswold

Peter Parley's Tales About America and Australia

Goodrich Samuel Griswold

Peter Parley's Tales About America and Australia

ISBN/EAN: 9783337315474

Printed in Europe, USA, Canada, Australia, Japan

Cover: Foto ©Andreas Hilbeck / pixelio.de

More available books at **www.hansebooks.com**

The Project Gutenberg eBook, Peter Parley's Tales About America and Australia, by Samuel Griswold Goodrich, Edited by Rev. T. Wilson, Illustrated by S. Williams

Title: Peter Parley's Tales About America and Australia

Author: Samuel Griswold Goodrich

Editor: Rev. T. Wilson

Release Date: October 17, 2005 [eBook #16891]

Language: English

Character set encoding: ISO-8859-1

START OF THE PROJECT GUTENBERG EBOOK PETER PARLEY'S TALES ABOUT AMERICA AND AUSTRALIA

E-text prepared by Robert Cicconetti, Janet Blenkinship, and the Project Gutenberg Online Distributed Proofreading Team (http://www.pgdp.net) from images generously made available by the University of Florida and the Internet Archive/Children's Library

Note: Images of the original pages are available through the Florida Board of Education, Division of Colleges and Universities, PALMM Project, 2001. (Preservation and Access for American and British Children's Literature, 1850-1869.) See
http://fulltext10.fcla.edu/cgi/t/text/text-idx?c=juv&idno=UF00003253&format=jpg
or
http://fulltext10.fcla.edu/cgi/t/text/text-idx?

8/15/12   The Project Gutenberg eBook of Peter Parley's Tales About America and Australia, by Samuel Griswold...

c=juv&idno=UF00003253&format=pdf

TALES

ABOUT

AMERICA AND AUSTRALIA.

BY

PETER PARLEY.

A New Edition,

BROUGHT DOWN TO THE PRESENT TIME.

REVISED BY

THE REV. T. WILSON.

WITH ILLUSTRATIONS BY S. WILLIAMS.

LONDON:
DARTON AND HODGE, HOLBORN HILL.
1862.

CONTENTS.

CHAPTER I.

PARLEY TELLS HOW AMERICA WAS FIRST DISCOVERED, AND ABOUT COLUMBUS THE DISCOVERER.

Now that I have given you an account of European cities in my "Tales about Europe," I shall now furnish you with some description of America, with its flourishing cities, and its multitude of ships, its fertile fields, its mighty rivers, its vast forests, and its millions of happy and industrious inhabitants, of which I am quite certain you must be very curious to know something, when you are told that though the world has been created nearly six thousand years, and many powerful nations have flourished and decayed, and are now scarcely remembered, yet it is only three hundred and seventy years ago since it was known that such a country as America existed.

It was in the year 1492, which you know is only 370 years since, on the third of August, a little before sunrise, that Christopher Columbus, undertaking the boldest enterprise that human genius ever conceived, or human talent and fortitude ever accomplished, set sail from Spain, for the discovery of the Western World.

I will now give you a short account of Columbus, who was one of the greatest men the world ever produced. He was born in the city of Genoa, in Italy; his family were almost all sailors, and he was brought up for a sailor also, and after being taught geography and various other things necessary for a sea captain to know, he was sent on board ship at the age of fourteen. Columbus was tall, muscular, and of a commanding aspect; his hair, light in youth, turned prematurely grey, and ere he reached the age of thirty was white as snow.

His first voyages were short ones, but after several years, desiring to see and learn more of distant countries, and thinking there were still new ones to be discovered, he went into the service of the King of Portugal and made many voyages to the western coast of Africa, and to the Canaries, and the Madeiras, and the Azores, islands lying off that coast, which were then the most westerly lands known to Europeans.

In his visits to these parts, one person informed him that his ship, sailing out farther to the west than usual, had picked up out of the sea a piece of wood curiously carved, and that very thick canes, like those which travellers had found in India, had been seen floating on the waves; also that great trees, torn up by the roots, had often been cast on shore, and once two dead bodies of men, with strange features, neither like Europeans nor Africans, were driven on the coast of the Azores.

All these stories set Columbus thinking and considering that these strange things had come drifting over the sea from the west, he looked upon them as tokens sent from some unknown countries lying far distant in that quarter: he was therefore eager to sail away and explore, but as he had not money enough himself to fit out ships and hire sailors, he determined to go and try to persuade some king or some state to be at the expense of the trial.

First he went to his own countrymen the Genoese, but they would have nothing to say to him: he then submitted his plan to the Portuguese, but the King of Portugal, pretending to listen to him, got from him his plan, and perfidiously attempted to rob him of the honour of accomplishing it, by sending another person to pursue the same track which he had proposed.

The person they so basely employed did not succeed, but returned to Lisbon, execrating a plan he had not abilities to execute.

On discovering this treachery, Columbus quitted the kingdom in disgust and set out for Spain, to King Ferdinand and Queen Isabella. He was now so poor that he was frequently obliged to beg as he went along.

About half a league from Palos, a sea-port of Andalusia in Spain, on a solitary height, overlooking the sea-coast, and surrounded by a forest of pines, there stood, and now stands at the present day, an ancient convent of Franciscan friars.

A stranger, travelling on foot, accompanied by a young boy, stopped one day at the gate of the convent, and asked of the porter a little bread and water for his child.—That stranger was Columbus, accompanied by his son Diego.

While receiving this humble refreshment, the guardian of the convent, Friar Juan Perez, happening to pass, was taken with the appearance of the stranger, and being an intelligent man and acquainted with geographical science, he became interested with the conversation of Columbus, and was so struck with the grandeur of his project that he detained him as his guest and invited a friend of his, Martin Alonzo Pinzon, a resident of the town of Palos, to come and hear Columbus explain his plan.

Pinzon was one of the most intelligent sea captains of the day, and a distinguished navigator. He not only approved of his project, but offered to engage in it, and to assist him.

Juan Perez now advised Columbus to repair to court. Pinzon generously furnished him with the money for the journey, and the friar kindly took charge of his youthful son Diego, to maintain and educate him in the convent, which I am sure you will think was the greatest kindness he could have done him at that time.

Ferdinand and Isabella gave him hopes and promises, then they made difficulties and objections, and would do nothing. At last, after waiting five years, he was just setting off for England, where he had previously sent his brother Bartholomew, when he was induced to wait a little longer in Spain.

This little longer was two years, but then at last he had his reward, for queen Isabella stood his friend, and even offered to part with her own jewels in order to raise money to enable him to make preparations for the voyage, so that he contrived to fit out three very small vessels which altogether carried but one hundred and twenty men.

Two of the vessels were light *barques*, or barges built high at the prow and stern, with forecastles and cabins for the crew, but were without deck in the centre; only one of the three, the Santa Maria, was completely decked; on board of this, Columbus hoisted his flag. Martin Alonzo Pinzon commanded the Pinta, and his brother, Vincente Yanez Pinzon, the Nina. He set sail in the sight of a vast crowd, all praying for the success, but never expecting and scarcely hoping to see either him or any of his crews again.

Columbus first made sail for the Canaries, where he repaired his vessels: then taking leave of these islands, he steered his course due west, across the great Atlantic ocean, where never ship had ploughed the waves before.

No sooner had they lost sight of land than the sailors' hearts began to fail them, and they bewailed themselves like men condemned to die: but Columbus cheered them with the hopes of the rich countries they were to discover.

After awhile they came within those regions where the trade-wind, as it is called, blows constantly from east to west without changing, which carried them on at a vast rate; but he judiciously concealed from his ignorant and timid crews the progress he made, lest they might be alarmed at the speed with which they were receding from home. After some time, they found the sea covered with weeds, as thick as a meadow with grass, and the sailors fancied that they should soon be stuck fast,—that they had reached the end of the navigable ocean, and that some strange thing would befal them.

Still, however, Columbus cheered them on, and the sight of a flock of birds encouraged them: but when they had been three weeks at sea and no land appeared, they grew desperate with fear, and plotted among themselves to force their commander to turn back again, lest all their provisions should be spent, or, if he refused, to throw him overboard.

Columbus, however, made them a speech which had such an effect upon them that they became tolerably quiet for a week longer; they then grew so violent again that at last he was obliged to promise them that if they did not see land in three days, he would consent to give it up and sail home again.

But he was now almost sure that land was not far off: the sea grew shallower, and early every morning flocks of land birds began to flutter around them, and these all left the ship in the evening, as if to roost on shore. One of the vessels had picked up a cane newly cut, and another a branch covered with fresh red berries; and the air blew softer and warmer, and the wind began to vary.

That very night, Columbus ordered the sails to be taken in, and strict watch to be kept, in all the ships, for fear of running aground; he and all his men remained standing on the deck, looking out eagerly: at length he spied a distant light; he showed it to two of his officers, and they all plainly perceived it moving, as if carried backwards and forwards, from house to house.

Soon after the cry of *"Land! land!"* was heard from the foremost ship, and, at dawn of day, they plainly saw a beautiful island, green and woody, and watered with many pleasant streams, lying stretched before them.

As soon as the sun rose, the boats of the vessel were lowered and manned, and Columbus, in a rich and splendid dress of scarlet, entered the principal one. They then rowed towards the island, with their colours displayed, and warlike music, and other martial pomp.

Columbus was the first to leap on shore, to kiss the earth, and to thank God on his knees: his men followed, and throwing themselves at his feet they all thanked him for leading them thither, and begged his forgiveness for their disrespectful and unruly behaviour.

CHAPTER II.

PARLEY DESCRIBES THE INHABITANTS.

The poor inhabitants, a simple and innocent people, with copper-coloured skins and long black hair, not curled, like the negroes, but floating on their shoulders, or bound in tresses round their heads, came flocking down to the beach and stood gazing in silent admiration.

The dress of the Spaniards, the whiteness of their skins, their beards, their arms, and the vast machines that seemed to move upon the waters with wings, which they supposed had, during the night, risen out of the sea, or come down from the clouds; the sound and flash of the guns, which they mistook for thunder and lightning: all these things appeared to them strange and surprising; they considered the Spaniards as children of the sun, and paid homage to them as gods.

The Europeans were hardly less amazed at the scene now before them. Every herb, and shrub, and tree, differed from those which flourished in Europe: the inhabitants appeared in the simple innocence of nature, entirely naked; their features were singular, but not disagreeable, and their manners gentle and timid.

The first act of Columbus was to take solemn and formal possession of the country in the name of his sovereign; this was done by planting the Spanish flag on the coast, and other ceremonies, which the poor natives looked upon with wonder, but could not understand.

Nor could there be an act of greater cruelty and injustice; for the Spaniards could not have any right to drive these gentle and peaceful inhabitants (as they afterwards did) from their peaceful abodes, which had been theirs and their fathers before them, perhaps for thousands of years, and in the end, utterly to destroy them, and take their land for themselves.

After performing this ceremony, of which Columbus himself could not foresee the consequences to the Indians, for he was very kind to them, he made them presents of trinkets and other trifles, with which they were greatly delighted, and brought him in return the fruits of their fields and groves, and a sort of bread called cassada, made from the root of the yuca; with whatever else their own simple mode of life might afford.

Columbus then returned to his ship, accompanied by many of the islanders in their boats, which they called canoes; these simple and undiscerning children of nature having no foresight of the calamities and desolation which awaited their country.

This island was called by the natives Guanahini, and by the Spaniards St. Salvador: it is one of that cluster of West India Islands called the Bahamas, and if you look on the map you will see that it is the very first island that would present itself to a ship sailing direct from Spain.

Columbus did not continue his voyage for some days, as he wished to give all his sailors an opportunity of landing and seeing the wonders of the new-discovered world, and to take in a fresh supply of water, in which they were cheerfully assisted by the natives, who took them to the clearest springs and the sweetest and freshest streams, filling their casks and rolling them to the boats, and seeking in every way to gratify (as they believed) their celestial visitors.

Columbus having thus refreshed his crews, and supplied his ships with water, proceeded on his voyage. After visiting several smaller islands he discovered a large island which the natives called Cuba, and which still retains that name. This was so large an island that he at first thought it to be a new continent.

In proceeding along the coast, having observed that most of the people whom he had seen wore small plates of gold by way of ornament in their noses, he eagerly inquired, by signs, where they got that precious metal.

The Indians, as much astonished at his eagerness in quest of gold as the Europeans were at their ignorance and simplicity, pointed towards the east, to an island which they called Hayti, in which this metal was more abundant.

Columbus ordered his squadron to bend their course thither, but Martin Alonzo Pinzon, impatient to be the first who should take possession of the treasure which this country was supposed to contain, quitted his companions with his ship, the Pinta, and though Columbus made signals to slacken sail, he paid no regard to them.

When they came in sight of Hayti, which you will see was no great distance, if you look on the map, Columbus having had no sleep the night before, had gone to his cabin to lie down and rest himself, having first given the charge of the vessel to an experienced sailor.

This careless man, (this lazy lubber, the sailors would call him,) instead of performing his duty, and watching over the safety of the ship and the lives of his companions, which were entrusted to him, deserted his post and went to sleep, leaving the vessel to the management of a young and thoughtless boy.

The rapid currents which prevail on that coast soon carried the vessel on a shoal, and Columbus was roused from his sleep by the striking of the ship and the cries of the terrified boy.

They first endeavoured, by taking out an anchor, to warp the vessel off, but the strength of the current was more than a match for them, and the vessel was driven farther and farther on the shoal; they then cut away the mast and took out some of the stores to lighten her; but all their efforts were vain.

Before sunset the next evening the vessel was a complete wreck. Fortunately the Nina was close at hand, and the shipwrecked mariners got on board of her; the inhabitants of the island came in their canoes and assisted them in preserving part of their stores.

They found Hayti a very beautiful island, and were treated with the greatest kindness by the inhabitants; but, though delighted with the beauty of the scenes which everywhere presented themselves, and amazed at the luxuriance and fertility of the soil, Columbus did not find gold in such quantities as was sufficient to satisfy the avarice of his followers; he was nevertheless anxious to prolong his voyage, and explore those magnificent regions which seemed to invite them on every hand.

But as the Pinta had never joined them again after parting from them, he had no vessel now left but the Nina; he did not therefore think it prudent to pursue his discoveries with one small vessel, and that a very crazy one, lest, if any accident should befal it, he might be left without the means of returning to Europe, and both the glory and benefit of his great discoveries might be lost; so he determined to prepare for his return.

But as it was impossible for so small a vessel as the Nina to contain the crew of the ship that was wrecked in addition to its own, Columbus was greatly perplexed what to do.

Many of his men were so delighted with the island and its inhabitants, that they begged of him to let them remain there, and Columbus consented to leave forty of them on the island, while he and the remainder made the voyage back.

He promised to return to them speedily. He now built them a fort with the timber of the wreck, and fortified it with the guns of the Santa Maria, and did every thing in his power to provide for their comfort during his absence, particularly enjoining them to be kind and peaceful towards the Indians.

This was the first colony of Europeans that settled in the new world, and Columbus gave it the name of Navidad.

CHAPTER III.

COLUMBUS SETS SAIL TO RETURN TO SPAIN, AND ENCOUNTERS A DREADFUL STORM.

Having obtained a certain quantity of the precious metals, and other curious productions of the countries he had discovered, he set sail to recross the wide Atlantic Ocean.

It was the second day after they had left the island that they saw a sail at a distance, which proved to be the Pinta.

On joining the admiral, Pinzon made many excuses and endeavoured to account for his desertion, saying he had been separated by stress of weather. Columbus admitted his excuse, but he ascertained afterwards that Pinzon parted company intentionally, and had steered directly east in quest of a region where the Indians had assured him that he would find gold in abundance.

They had guided him to Hayti, where he had been for some time, in a river about fifteen leagues from the part of the coast where Columbus had been wrecked.

He had collected a large quantity of gold by trading with the natives, and on leaving the river he had carried off four Indian men and two girls to be sold in Spain.

Columbus immediately sailed back for this river, and ordered the four men and two girls to be dismissed well clothed and with many presents, to atone for the wrong they had experienced. This resolution was not carried into effect without great unwillingness and many angry words on the part of Pinzon.

Columbus, being now joined by the Pinta, thought he might pursue his discoveries a little further, and on leaving this part of the coast he took with him four young Indians to guide him to the Carribean Islands, of which they gave him a very interesting account, as well as of another island said to be inhabited by Amazons.

A favourable breeze, however, sprang up for the voyage homewards, and seeing gloom and impatience in the countenances of his men, he gave up his intention of visiting these islands, and made all sail for Spain, the young Indians having consented to accompany him that they might learn the Spanish language, and be his guides and interpreters when they should return.

His voyage homeward was much more tedious; for those trade winds which had wafted him so rapidly westward, across the Atlantic, still blew from east to west, and Columbus did not then know that their influence only extends to a certain distance on each side of the Equator, so that if he had sailed a little farther north, on his return, he would very likely have met with a south-west wind, which was just what he wanted.

On the 12th of February they had made such progress as led them to hope they should soon see land. The wind now came on to blow violently; on the following evening there were three flashes of lightning in the north-east, from which signs Columbus predicted an approaching tempest.

It soon burst upon them with frightful violence. Their small and crazy vessels were little fitted for the wild storms of the Atlantic; all night they were obliged to scud under bare poles, at the mercy of the elements; as the morning dawned there was a transient pause and they made a little sail, but the wind rose with redoubled fury from the south and increased in the night, threatening each moment to overwhelm them or dash them to pieces.

The admiral made signal-lights for the Pinta to keep in company, but she was separated by the violence of the storm, and her lights gleamed more and more distant till they ceased entirely.

When the day dawned the sea presented a frightful waste of wild and broken waves. Columbus looked round anxiously for the Pinta, but she was nowhere to be seen, and he became apprehensive that Pinzon had borne away for Spain, that he might reach it before him, and by giving the first account of his discoveries, deprive him of his fame.

Through a dreary day the helpless bark was driven along by the tempest.

Seeing all human skill baffled and confounded, Columbus endeavoured to propitiate heaven by solemn vows, and various private vows were made by the seamen. The heavens, however, seemed deaf to their vows: the storm grew still more furious, and every one gave himself up for lost.

During this long and awful conflict of the elements, the mind of Columbus was a prey to the most distressing anxiety.

He was harassed by the repinings of his crew, who cursed the hour of their leaving their country.

He was afflicted also with the thought of his two sons, who would be left destitute by his death.

But he had another source of distress more intolerable than death itself. In case the Pinta should have foundered, as was highly probable, the history of his discovery would depend upon his own feeble bark. One surge of the ocean might bury it for ever in oblivion, and his name only be recorded as that of a desperate adventurer.

At this crisis, when all was given up for lost, Columbus had presence of mind enough to retire to his cabin and to write upon parchment a short account of his voyage.

This he wrapped in an oiled cloth, which he enclosed in a cake of wax, put it into a tight cask, and threw it into the sea, in hopes that some fortunate accident might preserve a deposit of so much importance to the world.

But that being which had preserved him through so many dangers still protected him; and happily these precautions were superfluous.

At sunset there was a streak of clear sky in the west; the wind shifted to that quarter, and on the morning of the 15th of February they came in sight of land.

The transports of the crew at once more beholding the old world, were almost equal to those they had experienced on discovering the new. This proved to be the island of St. Mary, the most southern of the Azores.

After remaining here a few days, the wind proving favourable he again set sail, on the 24th of February.

After two or three days of pleasant sailing, there was a renewal of tempestuous weather.

About midnight of the 2nd of March the caravel was struck by a squall, which rent all her sails and threatened instant destruction. The crew were again reduced to despair, and made vows of fasting and pilgrimages.

The storm raged through the succeeding day, during which, from various signs they considered that land must be near. The turbulence of the following night was dreadful; the sea was broken, wild, and mountainous, the rain fell in torrents, and the lightning flashed and the thunder pealed from various parts of the heavens.

In the first watch of this fearful night, the seamen gave the usual welcome cry of land—but it only increased their alarm, for they dreaded being driven on shore or dashed upon the rocks. Taking in sail, therefore, they endeavoured to keep to sea as much as possible. At day-break on the 4th of March they found themselves off the rock of Cintra at the mouth of the Tagus, which you know is the principal river of Portugal.

Though distrustful of the Portuguese, he had no alternative but to run in for shelter. The inhabitants came off from various parts of the shore to congratulate him on what they deemed a miraculous preservation, for they had been watching the vessel the whole morning with great anxiety, and putting up prayers for her safety. The oldest mariners of the place assured him that they had never during the whole course of their lives known so tempestuous a winter.

Such were the difficulties and perils with which Columbus had to contend on his return to Europe. Had one tenth part of them beset his outward voyage, his factious crew would have risen in arms against the enterprise, and he never would have discovered the new world.

The king of Portugal must have been greatly mortified when he heard of the arrival of Columbus and the wonderful discoveries he had made, for he could not but reflect that all the advantages of these discoveries might have belonged to him if he had not treated Columbus as he did.

But notwithstanding the envy which it was natural for the Portuguese to feel, he was allowed to come to Lisbon, and was treated with all the marks of distinction due to a man who had performed things so extraordinary and unexpected. The king admitted him into his presence, and listened with admiration to the account which he gave of his voyage, while Columbus enjoyed the satisfaction of being able to prove the solidity of his schemes to those very persons who had with disgraceful ignorance rejected them as the projects of a visionary adventurer.

Columbus was so impatient to return to Spain that he remained only five days in Lisbon. On the 15th of March he arrived at Palos, seven months and eleven days from the time when he set out from thence upon his voyage.

When the prosperous issue of it was known, when they beheld the strange people, the unknown animals, and singular productions brought from the countries he had discovered, the joy was unbounded; all the bells were rung, the cannons were fired, and he was welcomed with all the acclamations which the people are ever ready to bestow on great and glorious characters. They flocked in crowds to the harbour to see him land, and nothing but Columbus and the New World, as the Spaniards called it, was talked of.

He was desired by Ferdinand and Isabella in the most respectful terms to repair to court, that they might receive from his own mouth, an account of his wonderful discoveries.

On his arrival at Barcelona the king and queen received him clad in their royal robes, seated upon a throne, and surrounded by their nobles.

When he approached, they commanded him to take his seat upon a chair prepared for him, and to give a circumstantial account of his voyage, which he related with a gravity suitable to the dignity of the audience he addressed, and with that modesty which ever accompanies superior merit.

Every mark of honour that gratitude or admiration could suggest, was conferred upon him; his family was ennobled, and, as a mark of particular favour, Isabella appointed his son Diego, the boy, who, you remember, had been left at the convent, page to prince Juan, the heir apparent, an honour only granted to sons of persons of distinguished rank.

The king and queen, and, after their example, the courtiers treated him with all the respect paid to persons of the highest rank. Yet some of these courtiers were his bitterest enemies, and did every thing they could, in his absence, to poison the minds of the king and queen against him, and to cause his downfall.

The favour shown Columbus by the sovereigns insured him for a time the caresses of the nobility, for in court every one is eager to lavish attentions upon the man "whom the king delighteth to honour."

At one of the banquets which were given him occured the well known circumstance of the egg.

A shallow courtier present, impatient of the honours paid to Columbus, and meanly jealous of him as a foreigner, abruptly asked him, whether he thought that, in case he had not discovered the Indies, there would have been wanting men in Spain capable of the enterprise.

To this Columbus made no direct reply but, taking an egg, invited the company to make it stand on one end. Every one attempted it, but in vain; whereupon he struck it upon the table, broke one end, and left it standing on the broken part; illustrating, in this simple manner, that when he had once shown the way to the new world, nothing was easier than to follow it.

CHAPTER IV.

COLUMBUS PREPARES FOR ANOTHER VOYAGE.

Columbus was now anxious to set out on another voyage to proceed with his discoveries, and the king and queen gave orders that every thing should be done to further his wishes.

By his exertions a fleet of seventeen sail, large and small, was soon in a state of forwardness; labourers and artificers of all kinds were engaged for the projected colonies, and an ample supply was provided of whatever was necessary for the cultivation of the soil, the working of the mines, and for traffic with the natives.

He now found no difficulty in getting sailors to accompany him, and the account he gave of the countries he had discovered, and particularly the intelligence that they abounded with gold, excited the avarice and rapacity of the Spaniards, and numbers of needy adventurers of ruined fortunes and desperate circumstances, were eager to share in the spoil.

Many persons of distinction, thinking to become rich by the same means, also volunteered to enlist, and many got on board of the ships by stealth, so that about 1500 set sail in the fleet, though only a thousand were originally permitted to embark.

The departure of Columbus on his second voyage presented a brilliant contrast to his gloomy embarkation at Palos.

There were three large ships of heavy burden and fourteen smaller vessels, and the persons on board, instead of being regarded by the populace as devoted men, were looked upon with envy as favoured mortals, destined to golden regions and delightful climes, where nothing but wealth, and wonder, and enjoyment awaited them.

At sunrise the whole fleet was under sail, on the 13th of October he lost sight of the Island of Ferro, and, favoured by the trade winds, was borne pleasantly along, till, on the 2nd of November, a lofty island was descried to the west, to which he gave the name of Dominica, from having discovered it on the Lord's day.

As the ships moved gently onward, other islands arose to sight, one after another, covered with forests and enlivened by the flight of parrots and other tropical birds, while the whole air was sweetened by the fragrance of the breezes which passed over them.

In one of these islands, to which the Spaniards gave the name of Guadaloupe, they first met with the delicious fruit, the Anana or pine-apple.

Columbus now sailed in the direction of Hayti, to which he had given the name of Hispaniola, where he shortly arrived.

In passing along the coast he set on shore one of the young Indians who had been taken from that neighbourhood and had accompanied him to Spain. He dismissed him finely apparelled, and loaded with trinkets, thinking he would impress his countrymen with favourable feelings towards the Spaniards, but he never heard anything of him afterwards.

When he arrived on that part of the island where he had built the fort and taken leave of his companions, the evening growing dark, the land was hidden from their sight. Columbus watched for the dawn of day with the greatest anxiety; when at last the approach of the morning sun rendering the objects on shore visible, in the place where the fort had stood, nothing was to be seen. No human being was near, neither Indian nor European; he ordered a boat to be manned, and himself went, at the head of a party, to explore how things really were.

The crew hastened to the place where the fortress had been erected; they found it burnt and demolished, the palisades beaten down, and the ground strewed with broken chests and fragments of European garments.

The natives, at their approach, did not welcome them as they expected, like friends, but fled and concealed themselves as if afraid to be seen.

Columbus, at length, with some difficulty, by signs of peace and friendship, persuaded a few of them to come forth to him. From them he learned, that scarcely had he set sail for Spain, when all his counsels and commands faded from the minds of those who remained behind. Instead of cultivating the good-will of the natives, they endeavoured, by all kinds of wrongful means, to get possession of their golden ornaments and other articles of value, and seduce from them their wives and daughters, and had also quarrelled among themselves.

The consequences of this bad conduct were what might have been expected: some died by sickness caused by intemperance, some fell in brawls between themselves about their ill-gotten spoil, and others were cut off by the Indians, whom they had so shamefully treated, and who afterwards pulled dawn and burnt their fort.

The misfortunes which had befallen the Spaniards in the vicinity of this harbour threw a gloom over the place, and it was considered by the superstitious mariners as under some baneful influence. The situation was low and unhealthy, and not capable of improvement; Columbus therefore determined to remove the settlement.

With this view he made choice of a situation more healthy and commodious than that of Navidad, and having ordered the troops and the various persons to be employed in the colony to be immediately disembarked, together with the stores, ammunition, and all the cattle and live-stock, he traced out the plan of a town in a large plain near a spacious bay; and obliging every person to put his hand to the work, the houses were soon so far advanced as to afford them shelter, and forts were constructed for their defence.

This rising city, the first that Europeans founded in the new world, he named Isabella, in honour of his patroness the Queen of Castile.

As long as the Indians had any prospect that their sufferings might terminate by the voluntary departure of the invaders, they submitted in silence, and dissembled their sorrow; but now that the Spaniards had built a town—now that they had dug up the ground and planted it with corn—it became apparent that they came not to visit the country, but to settle in it.

They were themselves naturally so abstemious and their wants so few, that they were easily satisfied with the fruits of the island, which, with a handful of maize or a little of the insipid bread made of the cassava root, were sufficient for their support.

But it was with difficulty they could afford subsistence for the new guests. The Spaniards, though considered an abstemious people, appeared to them excessively voracious. One Spaniard consumed as much as several Indians; this keenness of appetite appeared so insatiable, that they supposed the Spaniards had left their own country because it did not produce enough to gratify their immoderate appetites, and had come among them in quest of nourishment.

Columbus having taken all the steps which he thought necessary to ensure the prosperity of his new colony, entrusted the command of the military force to Margaritta, and set sail with three vessels to extend his discoveries; but, after a long and tedious voyage, in which he endured every hardship, the most important discovery he made was the island of Jamaica.

Having been absent much longer than he had expected, he returned to his new settlement, but the colonists had become refractory and unmanageable.

No sooner had he left the island on his voyage of discovery, than the soldiers under Margaritta dispersed in straggling parties over the island, lived at discretion upon the natives, wasted their property, and treated that inoffensive race with the insolence of military oppression.

During the absence of Columbus, several unfavourable accounts of his conduct had been transmitted to Spain, and these accusations gained such credit in that jealous court, that Aguado, a person in every way unsuited for the purpose, was appointed to proceed to Hispaniola to observe the conduct of Columbus.

This man listened with eagerness to every accusation of the discontented Spaniards, and fomented still further the spirit of dissension in the island.

Columbus felt how humiliating it must be if he remained in the island with such a partial inspector to observe his motions and control his authority; he therefore took the resolution of returning to Spain, in order to lay a full account of his transactions before Ferdinand and Isabella.

Having committed the government of the colony during his absence to Don Bartholomew, his brother, he appointed Roldan Chief Justice, a choice which afterwards caused great calamities to the colony.

On his arrival in Spain, Columbus appeared at court with the confidence of a man, not only conscious of having done no wrong, but of having performed great services.

Ferdinand and Isabella, ashamed of having listened to ill-founded accusations, received him with such marks of respect as silenced the calumnies of his enemies, and covered them with shame and confusion.

The gold, the pearls, and other commodities of value which he had brought home, and the mines which he had found, fully proved the value and importance of his discoveries, though Columbus considered them only as preludes to future and more important acquisitions.

CHAPTER V.

PARLEY TELLS HOW COLUMBUS DISCOVERS THE CONTINENT OF AMERICA.

Columbus, having been furnished with six vessels of no great burden, departed on his third voyage. He touched at the Canaries and at the Cape de Verd islands; from the former he despatched three ships with a supply of provisions for the colony of Hispaniola; with the other three he continued his voyage to the south.

Nothing remarkable occurred till they were within five degrees of the line; then they were becalmed, and the heat became so excessive, that the wine casks burst and their provisions were spoiled.

The Spaniards, who had never ventured so far to the south, were afraid the ships would take fire, but they were relieved in some measure from their fear by a seasonable fall of rain.

This, however, though so heavy and incessant that the men could hardly keep the deck, did not greatly mitigate the heat, and Columbus was at last constrained to yield to the importunities of his crew, and to alter his course to the north-west, in order to reach some of the Caribbee islands, where he might refit and be supplied with provisions.

On the 1st of August, 1498, the man stationed at the round-top surprised them with the joyful cry of "Land!" They stood towards it, and discovered a considerable island, which the admiral called Trinidad, a name it still retains, and near it the mouth of a river, rolling towards the ocean such a vast body of water, and rushing into it with such impetuous force, that when it meets the tide, which on that coast rises to an uncommon height, their meeting occasions an extraordinary and dangerous swell of the waves.

In this conflict, the irresistable torrent of the river so far prevails, that it freshens the ocean many leagues with its flood.

Columbus, before he could perceive the danger, was entangled among these adverse currents and tempestuous waves; and it was with the utmost difficulty that he escaped through a narrow strait, which appeared so tremendous, that he called it "The Dragon's Mouth."

As soon as his consternation permitted him to reflect on an appearance so extraordinary, he justly concluded that the land must be a part of some mighty continent, and not of an island, because all the springs that could rise, and all the rain that could fall on an island, could never, as he calculated, supply water enough to feed so prodigiously broad and deep a river; and he was right, the river was the Oronoko.

Filled with this idea, he stood to the west, along the coast of those provinces which are now known by the name of Paria and Cumana. He landed in several places, and found the people to resemble those of Hispaniola in their appearance and manner of life.

They wore as ornaments small plates of gold and pearls of considerable value, which they willingly exchanged for European toys. They seemed to possess greater courage and better understandings than the inhabitants of the islands.

The country produced four-footed animals of several kinds, as well as a great variety of fowls and fruits.

The admiral was so much delighted with its beauty and fertility, that, with the warm enthusiasm of a discoverer, he imagined it to be the Paradise described in Scripture.

Thus Columbus had the glory of discovering the new world, and of conducting the Spaniards to that vast continent which has been the seat of their empire and the source of their treasure, in that quarter of the globe. The shattered condition of his ships and the scarcity of provisions, made it now necessary to bear away for Hispaniola, where he arrived wasted to an extreme degree with fatigue and sickness.

Many revolutions had happened in that country during his absence, which had lasted more than two years.

His brother, whom he had left in command, had, in compliance with advice which he had given him before his departure, removed the colony from Isabella to a more commodious station on the opposite side of the island, and laid the foundation of St. Domingo, which long continued to be the most considerable town in the new world.

Such was the cruelty and oppression with which the Spaniards treated the Indians, and so intolerable the burden imposed upon them, that they at last took arms against their oppressors; but these insurrections were not formidable. In a conflict with timid and naked Indians, there was neither danger nor doubt of victory.

A mutiny which broke out among the Spaniards, was of a more dangerous nature, the ringleader in which was Francisco Roldan, whom Columbus, when he sailed for Spain, had appointed chief judge, and whose duty it was to have maintained the laws, instead of breaking them.

This rebellion of Roldan, which threatened the whole country with ruin, was only subdued by the most wise and prudent conduct on the part of Columbus; but order and tranquillity were at length apparently restored.

As soon as his affairs would permit, he sent some of his ships to Spain, with a journal of the voyage which he had made, and a description of the new continent which he had discovered, and also a chart of the coast along which he had sailed, and of which I shall have something more to tell you presently.

He at the same time sent specimens of the gold, the pearls, and other curious and valuable productions which he had acquired by trafficking with the natives.

He also transmitted an account of the insurrection in Hispaniola, and accused the mutineers of having, by their unprovoked rebellion, almost ruined the colony.

Roldan and his associates took care to send to Spain, by the same ships, apologies for their mutinous conduct, and unfortunately for the happiness of Columbus, their story gained most credit in the court of Ferdinand and Isabella.

By these ships Columbus granted the liberty of returning to Spain to all those, who, from sickness or disappointment, were disgusted with the country. A good number of such as were most dissatisfied, embraced this opportunity of returning to Europe. The disappointment of their unreasonable hopes inflamed their rage against Columbus to the utmost pitch, and their distress made their accusations be believed.

A gang of these disorderly ruffians, who had been shipped off to free the island from their seditions, found their way to the court at Grenada. Whenever the king or queen appeared in public, they surrounded them, insisting, with importunate clamours, on the payment of arrears due to them, and demanding vengeance on the author of their sufferings.

These endeavours to ruin Columbus were seconded by Fonseca, who was now made bishop of Badajos, and who was entrusted with the chief direction of Indian affairs. This man had always been an implacable enemy of Columbus, and with others of his enemies who were about the court, having continual access to the sovereign, they were enabled to aggravate all the complaints that were urged against him, while they carefully suppressed his vindications of himself.

By these means Ferdinand was at last induced to send out Bobadilla, an officer of the royal household, to inquire into the conduct of Columbus, and if he should think the charges against him proved, to supersede him in his command, that is, to send him home, and make himself governor in his stead; so that it was the interest of the judge to pronounce the person guilty whom he was sent to try.

On his arrival he found Columbus absent in the interior of the island; and as he had, before he landed, made up his mind to treat him as a criminal, he proceeded at once, without any inquiry, to supersede him in his command.

He took up his residence in Columbus' house, from which the owner was absent, seized upon his arms, gold, plate, jewels, books, and even his letters and most secret manuscripts, giving no account of the property thus seized, but disposing of it as if already confiscated to the crown; at the same time he used the most unqualified language when speaking of Columbus, and hinted that he was empowered to send him home in chains; thus acting as if he had been sent out to degrade the admiral, not to inquire into his conduct.

As soon as Columbus arrived from the interior, Bobadilla gave orders to put him in irons and confine him in the fortress, and so far from hearing him in his defence, he would not even admit him to his presence; but having collected from his enemies what he thought sufficient evidence, he determined to send both him and his brother home in chains.

The charge of conducting the prisoners to Spain was committed to Alonzo Villejo, a man of honourable conduct and generous feelings. When Villejo entered with the guard to conduct him on board the caravel, Columbus thought it was to conduct him to the scaffold. "Villejo" said he, "whither are you taking me?" "To the ship, your excellency, to embark," replied the other. "To embark!" repeated the admiral, earnestly, "Villejo, do you speak the truth?" "By the life of your excellency," replied the honest officer, "it is true."

With these words the admiral was comforted, and felt as restored from death to life, for he now knew he should have an opportunity of vindicating his conduct. The caravel set sail in October, bearing off Columbus shackled like the vilest criminal.

The worthy Villejo, as well as Andries Martin, the master of the caravel, would have taken off his irons, but to this he would not consent. "No," said he proudly, "their majesties commanded me, by letter, to submit to whatever Bobadilla should order in their name; by their authority he has put upon me these chains; I will wear them till they shall order them to be taken off, and I will afterwards preserve them as relics and memorials of the reward of my services."

The arrival of Columbus, a prisoner and in chains, produced almost as great a sensation as his triumphant return on his first voyage.

A general burst of indignation arose in Cadiz and in Seville, which was echoed through all Spain, that Columbus was brought home in chains from the world he had discovered.

The tidings reached the court of Grenada, and filled the halls of the Alhambra with murmurs of astonishment.

On the arrival of the ships at Cadiz, Columbus, full of his wrongs, but not knowing how far they had been authorized by his sovereigns, forbare to write to them; but he sent a long letter to a lady of the court, high in favour with the queen, containing, in eloquent and touching language, an ample vindication of his conduct.

When it was read to the noble-minded Isabella, and she found how grossly Columbus had been wronged, and the royal authority abused, her heart was filled with sympathy and indignation.

Without waiting for any documents that might arrive from Bobadilla, Ferdinand and Isabella sent orders to Cadiz, that he should be instantly set at liberty, and treated with all distinction, and sent him two thousand ducats to defray his expenses to court. They wrote him a letter at the same time, expressing their grief at all that had happened, and inviting him to Grenada.

He was received by their majesties with the greatest favour and distinction. When the queen beheld this venerable man approach, and thought on all he had deserved and all he had suffered, she was moved to tears.

Columbus had borne up firmly against the injuries and wrongs of the world, but when he found himself thus kindly treated, and beheld tears in the benign eyes of Isabella, his long suppressed feelings burst forth, he threw himself upon his knees, and for some time could not utter a word for the violence of his tears and sobbings.

Ferdinand and Isabella raised him from the ground and endeavoured to encourage him by the most gracious expressions.

As soon as he had recovered his self-possession, he entered into an eloquent and high-minded vindication of his conduct, and his zeal for the glory and advantage of the Spanish crown.

The king and queen expressed their indignation at the proceedings of Bobadilla, and promised he should be immediately dismissed from his command.

The person chosen to supersede Bobadilla was Nicholas de Ovando. While his departure was delayed by various circumstances, every arrival brought intelligence of the disasterous state of the island under the administration of Bobadilla.

He encouraged the Spaniards in the exercise of the most wanton cruelties towards the natives, to obtain from them large quantities of gold. "Make the most of your time," he would say, "there is no knowing how long it will last;" and the colonists were not backward in following his advice. In the meantime the poor Indians sunk under the toils imposed upon them, and the severities with which they were enforced.

These accounts hastened the departure of Ovando, and a person sailed with him, in order to secure what he could of the wreck of Columbus' property.

CHAPTER VI.

PARLEY TELLS HOW COLUMBUS WAS ROBBED OF THE HONOUR OF GIVING HIS NAME TO AMERICA.

I have told you that Columbus, as soon as he arrived at Hispaniola, after discovering the new continent, sent a ship to Spain with a journal of the voyage he had made, and a description of the new continent which he had discovered, together with a chart of the coast of Paria and Cumana, along which he had sailed.

This journal, with the charts and description, and Columbus' letters on the subject, were placed in the custody of Fonseca, he being minister for Indian affairs.

No sooner had the particulars of this discovery been communicated by Columbus, than a separate commission of discovery, signed by Fonseca, but not by the sovereigns, was granted to Alonzo de Ojeda, who had accompanied Columbus on his second voyage, and whom Columbus had instructed in all his plans. Ojeda was accompanied on this voyage by a Florentine, whose name was Amerigo Vespucci.

To these adventurers Fonseca communicated Columbus' journal, his description of the country, his charts, and all his private letters.

This expedition sailed from Spain while Columbus was still at Hispaniola, and wholly ignorant of what was taking place; and Ojeda, without touching at the colony, steered his course direct for Paria, following the very track which Columbus had marked out.

Having extended their discoveries very little farther than Columbus had gone before them, Vespucci, on returning to Spain, published an account of his adventures and discoveries, and had the address and confidence so to frame his narrative, as to make it appear that the glory of having discovered the new continent belonged to him.

Thus the bold pretensions of an impostor have robbed the discoverer of his just reward, and the caprice of fame has unjustly assigned to him an honour far above the renown of the greatest conquerors—that of indelibly impressing his name upon this vast portion of the earth, which ought in justice to have been called Columbia.

Two years had now been spent in soliciting the favour of an ungrateful court, and notwithstanding all his merits and services, he solicited in vain; but even this ungracious return did not lessen his ardour in his favourite pursuits, and his anxiety to pursue those discoveries in which he felt he had yet only made a beginning.

Ferdinand at last consented to grant him four small vessels, the largest of which did not exceed seventy tons in burden; but, accustomed to brave danger and endure hardships, he did not hesitate to accept the command of this pitiful squadron, and he sailed from Cadiz on his fourth voyage on the 9th of May.

Having touched, as usual, at the Canaries, he intended to have sailed direct for this new discovered continent; but his largest vessel was so clumsy and unfit for service, that he determined to bear away for Hispaniola, in hopes of exchanging her for some ship of the fleet that had carried out Ovando.

The fleet that had brought out Ovando lay in the harbour ready to put to sea, and was to take home Bobadilla, together with Roldan and many of his adherents, to be tried in Spain for rebellion. Bobadilla was to embark in the principal ship, on board of which he had put an immense amount of gold, which he hoped would atone for all his faults.

Among the presents intended for his sovereign was one mass of virgin gold, which was famous in the Spanish chronicles; it was said to weigh 3600 castillanos. Large quantities of gold had been shipped in the fleet by Roldan and other adventurers—the wealth gained by the sufferings of the unhappy natives.

Columbus sent an officer on shore to request permission to shelter his squadron in the river, as he apprehended an approaching storm. He also cautioned them not to let the fleet sail, but his request was refused by Ovando, and his advice disregarded.

The fleet put to sea, and Columbus kept his feeble squadron close to shore, and sought for shelter in some wild bay or river of the island.

Within two days, one of those tremendous storms which sometimes sweep those latitudes gathered up, and began to blow. Columbus sheltered his little squadron as well as he could, and sustained no damage. A different fate befel the other armament.

The ship in which were Bobadilla, Roldan, and a number of the most inveterate enemies of Columbus, was swallowed up with all its crew, together with the principal part of the ill-gotten treasure, gained by the miseries of the Indians.

Some of the ships returned to St. Domingo, and only one was able to continue her voyage to Spain; that one had on board four thousand pieces of gold, the property of Columbus, which had been recovered by the agent whom he sent out with Ovando.

Thus, while the enemies of the admiral were swallowed up as it were before his eyes, the only ship enabled to pursue her voyage was the frail bark freighted with his property.

CHAPTER VII.

PARLEY TELLS HOW COLUMBUS WAS SHIPWRECKED, AND ALSO OF THE MANNER OF HIS DEATH.

Columbus soon left Hispaniola where he met with so inhospitable a reception, and steering towards the west, he arrived on the coast of Honduras. There he had an interview with some of the inhabitants of the continent, who came off in a large canoe; they appeared to be more civilized than any whom he had hitherto discovered.

In return to the inquiries which the Spaniards made with their usual eagerness, where the Indians got the gold which they wore by way of ornaments, they directed him to countries situated to the west, in which gold was found in such profusion that it was applied to the most common uses.

Well would it have been for Columbus had he followed their advice. Within a day or two he would have arrived at Yucatan; the discovery of Mexico and the other opulent countries of New Spain would have necessarily followed, the Southern Ocean would have been disclosed to him, and a succession of splendid discoveries would have shed fresh glory on his declining age.

But the admiral's mind was bent upon discovering the supposed strait that was to lead to the Indian Ocean. In this navigation he explored a great extent of coast from Cape Gracios à Dios till he came to a harbour, which on account of its beauty and security, he called Porto Bello.

On quitting this harbour he steered for the south, and he had not followed this course many days when he was overtaken by storms more terrible than any he had yet encountered.

For nine days the vessels were tossed about at the mercy of a raging tempest. The sea, according to the description of Columbus, boiled at times like a cauldron, at other times it ran in mountain waves covered with foam: at night the raging billows sparkled with luminous particles, which made them resemble great surges of flame.

For a day and a night the heavens glowed like a furnace with incessant flashes of lightning, while the loud claps of thunder were often mistaken for signal guns of their foundering companions.

In the midst of this wild tumult of the elements, they beheld a new object of alarm. The ocean, in one place, became strangely agitated; the water was whirled up into a kind of pyramid or cone; while a livid cloud, tapering to a point, bent down to meet it; joining together, they formed a column, which rapidly approached the ship, spinning along the surface of the deep, and drawing up the water with a rushing sound, it passed the ship without injury.

His leaky vessels were not able to withstand storms like these. One of them foundered, and he was obliged to abandon another.

With the remaining two he bore away for Hispaniola, but in the tempest his ships falling foul of each other, it was with the greatest difficulty he reached the island of Jamaica.

His two vessels were in such a shattered condition, that, to prevent them from sinking, and to save the lives of his crews, he was obliged to run them on shore.

Having no ship now left, he had no means of reaching Hispaniola, or of making his situation known. In this juncture he had recourse to the hospitable kindness of the natives, who, considering the Spaniards as beings of a superior nature, were eager, on every occasion to assist them.

From them he obtained two canoes, each formed out of a single tree hollowed with fire. In these, which were only fit for creeping along the coast, two of his brave and faithful companions, assisted by a few Indians, gallantly offered to set out for Hispaniola; this voyage they accomplished in ten days, after encountering incredible fatigues and dangers.

By them he wrote letters to Ovando, describing his situation and requesting him to send ships to bring off him and his crews; but what will you think of the unfeeling cruelty of this man, when I tell you that he suffered these brave men to wait eight months before he would give them any hopes of relieving their companions: and what must have been the feelings of Columbus during this period.

At last the ships arrived which were to take them from the island, where the unfeeling Ovando had suffered them to languish above a year, exposed to misery in all its various forms. When he arrived at St. Domingo, Ovando treated him with every kind of insult and injustice. Columbus submitted in silence, but became extremely impatient to quit a country where he had been treated with such barbarity.

The preparations were soon finished, and he set sail for Spain with two ships, but disaster still pursued him to the end of his course. He suffered acutely from a painful and dangerous disease, and his mind was kept uneasy and anxious by a continued succession of storms. One of the vessels being disabled, was forced back to St. Domingo, and in the other he sailed 700 leagues with jury-masts, and reached with difficulty the port of St. Lucar in Spain, 1504.

On his arrival he received the fatal news of the death of his patroness queen Isabella, from whom he had hoped for the redress of his wrongs.

He applied to the king, who, instead of confirming the titles and honours which he had formerly conferred upon him, insulted him with the proposal of renouncing them all for a pension.

Disgusted with the ingratitude of a monarch whom he had served with fidelity and success, exhausted with the calamities which he had endured, and broken with infirmities, this great and good man breathed his last at Valladolid, A.D. 1506, in the 69th year of his age.

He was buried in the cathedral at Seville, and on his tomb was engraved an epitaph commemorating his discovery of a New World.

Christobal Colon, obiit 1506,

Ætat 69.

A Castilla y a Leon
Neubo Mundo dio Colon.[A]

Thus much for Columbus; those who are the greatest benefactors of mankind seldom meet with much gratitude from men in their lives; they must look to God for their reward, and leave future generations to do justice to their memory.

It was very unfortunate for the natives of America, that the country fell into the hands of such a cruel, covetous, and bigoted nation as the Spaniards were. Their thirst for gold was insatiable, and the cruelties they exercised upon the natives are too horrible to recite. After the death of Columbus, the Indians were no longer treated with gentleness, for it was his defence of the property and lives of these harmless natives that brought down upon his head such bitter hatred. You will now look into your map and follow Columbus in some of his discoveries. You will see a great number of islands extending in a curve from Florida, which is the southernmost part of the United States, to the mouth of the river Oronoko in South America; and, as Columbus firmly believed these islands, when he discovered them, to be a part of India, the name of Indies was given to them by Ferdinand and Isabella; and, even after the error was detected, and the true position of the new world ascertained, the name has remained, and the appellation of Indies is given to the country, and that of Indians to the inhabitants.

[A]   To Castile and to Leon Columbus gave a New World.

CHAPTER VIII.

PARLEY TELLS OF OVANDO'S CRUEL TREATMENT OF ANACAONA, THE PRINCESS OF HAYTI.

Columbus discovered and gave names to some of these islands, and on several of them he settled colonies, and did all he could to make them the abodes of peace and happiness.

On his taking leave of them for the last time, Ovando continued governor of Hayti.

The cruelties exercised by this unfeeling man it would take a volume to describe, but I will mention only one or two instances.

When the natives were unable to pay the tribute which he exacted from them, he always accused them of insurrection, and it was to punish a slight insurrection of this kind in the eastern part of the island that he sent his troops, who ravaged the country with fire and sword. He showed no mercy to age or sex, putting many to death with horrible tortures, and brought off the brave Catabanama, one of the five sovereign caziques of the island, in chains to St. Domingo, where he was ignominiously hanged by Ovando, for the crime of defending his territory and his native soil against usurping strangers.

But the most atrocious act of Ovando, and one that must heap odium on his name, wherever the woes of the gentle natives of Hayti are heard of, was the cruelty he was guilty of towards the province of Xaragua for one of those pretended conspiracies.

Ovando set out at the head of nearly four hundred well armed soldiers, seventy of whom were steel-clad horsemen; giving out that he was coming on a visit of friendship, to make arrangements for the payment of tribute.

Behechio, the ancient cazique of the province, was dead, and his sister, Anacaona, wife of the late formidable chief Caonabo, had succeeded to the government.

She was one of the most beautiful females in the island; of great natural grace and dignity, and superior intelligence; her name in the Indian language signified "Golden Flower."

She came forth to meet Ovando, according to the custom of her nation, attended by her most distinguished subjects, and her train of damsels waving palm branches, and dancing to the cadence of their popular ayretos.

All her principal caziques had been assembled to do honour to the guests, who, for several days were entertained with banquets, and national games and dances.

In return for these exhibitions, Ovando invited Anacaona, with her beautiful daughter Higuenamata, and her principal subjects, to witness a tilting match in the public square.

When all were assembled, and the square crowded with unarmed Indians, Ovando gave a signal, and instantly the horsemen rushed into the midst of the naked and defenceless throng, trampling them under foot, cutting them down with their swords, transfixing them with their lances, and sparing neither age nor sex.

Above eighty caziques had been assembled in one of the principal houses: it was surrounded by troops, the caziques were bound to the posts which supported the roof, and put to cruel tortures, until in the extremity of anguish they were made to admit as true what their queen and themselves had been charged with.

When they had thus been made, by torture, to accuse themselves, a horrible punishment was immediately inflicted. Fire was set to the house, and they all perished miserably in the flames.

As to Anacaona, she was carried to St. Domingo, where, after the mockery of a trial, she was pronounced guilty on the testimony of the Spaniards, and was barbarously hanged by the people whom she had so long and so greatly befriended.

After the massacre of Xaragua, the destruction of its inhabitants went on. They were hunted for six months amid the fastnesses of the mountains, and their country ravaged by horse and foot, until, all being reduced to deplorable misery and abject submission, Ovando pronounced the province restored to order; and in remembrance of his triumph, founded a town near the lake, which he called Santa Maria de la Verdadera Pas (St. Mary of the true peace.)

Such was the tragical fate of the beautiful Anacaona, once extolled as the Golden Flower of Hayti; and such the story of the delightful region of Xaragua, which the Spaniards, by their own account, found a perfect paradise, but which, by their vile passions, they filled with horror and desolation.

After this work of destruction, they made slaves of the remaining inhabitants, and divided them amongst them, and many of the sanguinary contests among themselves arose out of quarrels about the distribution.

We cannot help pausing to cast back a look of pity and admiration over these beautiful but devoted regions.

The white man had penetrated the land! In his train came avarice, pride, and ambition; sordid care, and pining labour, were soon to follow, and the paradise of the Indian was about to disappear for ever.

CHAPTER IX.

PARLEY DESCRIBES THE TREES, PLANTS, AND FLOWERS OF THE NEW WORLD.

When once the way had been pointed out, it was easy for other navigators to follow, and accordingly many Spaniards undertook voyages of further discovery.

Among others, Yanez Pinzon, one of the brave companions of Columbus, undertook a voyage to the new world in 1499.

This navigator suffered much from storms, and having sailed southward, he crossed the equator and lost sight of the polar star.

The sailors were exceedingly alarmed at this circumstance, as the polar star was relied upon by them as one of their surest guides; not knowing the shape of the earth, they thought that some prominence hid this star from their view.

The first land that Pinzon discovered, after crossing the line, was Cape St. Augustine, in eight degrees south latitude, the most projecting part of the extensive country of Brazil.

As the fierceness of the natives made it unsafe to land on this coast, he continued his voyage to the north-west, and fell in with the mighty river Amazon, which is nearly under the equinoctial line.

The mouth of this river is more than thirty leagues in breadth, and its waters enter more than forty leagues into the ocean without losing its freshness.

He now recrossed the line, and coming again in sight of the polar star, he pursued his course along the coast, passed the mouth of the Oronoko, and entered the Gulph of Paria, after which he returned to Spain.

Ojeda also undertook a voyage expressly to found a settlement; but as the character of the Spaniards was now well known to the inhabitants of these parts, they determined to oppose their landing, and being a numerous and warlike people, Ojeda nearly lost his life in the attempt.

Many of his companions were slain; the survivors, however, succeeding in making good their retreat on board the ships.

Shortly afterwards he landed on the eastern side of the Gulph of Darien, and built a fortress which they called San Sebastian.

Ojeda had with him in this expedition Francisco Pizarro, about whom I shall have to tell you something more presently.

About the same time another Spaniard, of the name of Nicuessa, formed a settlement on that part of the coast, and built a fortress there, which he called Nombre de Dios, not very distant from the harbour of Portobello.

Thus, by degrees, the whole coast of America, on the side of the Atlantic, was discovered and explored.

But the Spaniards did not know that in the part where they were, it was only a narrow neck of land (which you know is called an Isthmus) that separated them from another vast ocean; and this, when they discovered the ocean on the other side, was called the Isthmus of Darien.

I will now give you a short account of the discovery of this ocean.

Nothing having been heard of Ojeda and his new colony of San Sebastian, another expedition, commanded by Enciso, set sail in search of them.

Among the ship's company was a man, by name Vasco Ninez de Balboa, who, although of a rich family, had, by his bad habits, not only become very poor, but also very much in debt.

To avoid being thrown into prison for the debts that he owed, he contrived to get on board Enciso's ship, concealed in a cask, which was taken on board the vessel as a cask of provisions.

When the ship was far from St. Domingo, Balboa came out from his cask to the astonishment of all on board.

Enciso at first was angry at the way he had escaped from the punishment which his bad conduct had deserved; yet, as he thought that he might be of service to him, he pardoned him.

The settlement of St. Sebastian, however, had been broken up, the Spaniards having suffered much from the repeated attacks of the natives, who would no longer patiently submit to their unjust treatment.

Soon after Enciso arrived at Carthagena he was joined by Pizarro, with the wretched remains of the colony; he determined nevertheless, to continue his voyage to the settlement.

Upon his arrival there he found Pizarro's account was too true, for where St. Sebastian had stood, nothing was to be seen but a heap of ruins.

Here misfortune followed misfortune, his own ship was wrecked and then he was attacked by the natives.

In despair at these disasters Enciso was at a loss what to do, or where to go, when Balboa advised him to continue his course along the coast in Pizarro's little vessel.

He stated that he had once before been on an expedition in this same gulf, and on the western side he well remembered an Indian village, on the banks of a river, called by the natives Darien.

Enciso pleased with Balboa's advice, resolved to take possession of this village, and to drive out all the Indians.

Arrived at the river, he landed his men, and, without giving the unfortunate people of the village any notice, he attacked them, killed several, drove the rest out, and robbed them of all their possessions.

He then made the village the chief place of his new government, and called it Santa Maria del Darien. Balboa assisted in this work of cruelty and injustice.

The Spaniards had not been long here when they became tired with Enciso, and they refused to obey him, and sent him off in a ship to Spain. Upon his departure, Balboa took the command.

In one of his expeditions into the interior parts of the country in search of gold, he first heard of a sea to the west, as yet unknown to Europeans.

He had received a large quantity of gold from an Indian cazique, or chief, and was weighing it into shares for the purpose of dividing it among his men when a quarrel arose as to the exactness of the weight.

One of the sons of the Indian cazique was present, and he felt so disgusted at the sordid behaviour of the Spaniards that he struck the scales with his fist and scattered the glittering gold about the place.

Before the Spaniards could recover from their astonishment at this sudden act, he said to them, "why should you quarrel for such a trifle? If you really esteem gold to be so precious as to abandon your homes, and come and seize the lands and dwellings of others for the sake of it, I can tell you of a land not far distant where you may find it in plenty."

"Beyond those lofty mountains," he continued, pointing to the south, "lies a mighty sea, all the streams that flow into which down the southern side of those mountains, abound in gold, and all the utensils the people have, are made of gold."

Balboa was struck with this account of the young Indian, and eagerly inquired the best way of penetrating to this sea, and this land of gold.

The young Indian warned him of the dangers he would meet with from the fierce race of Indians inhabiting these mountains, who were cannibals, or eaters of human flesh, but Balboa was not to be deterred by accounts of difficulties and dangers.

He was, besides, desirous of getting possession of the gold, and of obtaining, by the merits of the discovery, the pardon of the King of Spain, for taking from Enciso the command of the settlement.

He resolved, therefore, to penetrate to this sea, and immediately began to make preparations for the journey.

He first sent to Hispaniola for an additional number of soldiers, to assist him in the perilous adventure, but instead of receiving these, the only news that reached him by the return of his messengers was, that he would most probably have the command of Darien taken from him, and be punished for assisting to dispossess Enciso.

This news made him determine no longer to delay his departure. All the men he could muster for the expedition amounted only to one hundred and ninety; but these were hardy and resolute, and much attached to him. He armed them with swords and targets; cross-bows and arquebusses; besides this little band, Balboa took with him a few of the Indians of Darien whom he had won by kindness, to serve him.

On the 1st of September, 1513, Balboa set out from Darien, first to the residence of the Indian cazique, from whose son he first heard of the sea.

From this chief he obtained the assistance of guides and some warriors, and with this force he prepared to penetrate the wilderness before him.

It was on the 6th of September that he began his march for the mountains which separated him from the great Pacific Ocean, he set out with a resolution to endure patiently all the miseries, and to combat boldly all the difficulties that he might meet with, and he contrived to rouse the same determination in his followers.

Their journey was through a broken rocky country covered with forest trees and underwood, so thick and close as to be quite matted together and every here and there deep foaming streams, some of which they were forced to cross on rafts.

So wearisome was the journey, that in four days they had not advanced more than ten leagues, and they began to suffer much from hunger.

They had now arrived in the province of a warlike tribe of Indians who, instead of flying and hiding themselves, came forth to the attack. They set upon the Spaniards with furious yells, thinking to overpower them at once. They were armed with bows and arrows, and clubs made of palm-wood almost as hard as iron. But the first shock of the report from the fire-arms of the Spaniards struck them with terror. They took to flight, but were closely pursued by the Spaniards with their blood-hounds. The Cazique and six hundred of his people were left dead upon the field of battle.

After the battle the Spaniards entered the adjoining village, which was at the foot of the last mountain that remained to be climbed; this village they robbed of every thing valuable. There was much gold and many jewels.

Balboa shared the booty among his band of followers. But this victory was not gained without some loss on the side of the Spaniards.

Balboa found that several of his men had been wounded by the arrows of the Indians, and many also, overcome with fatigue, had fallen sick, these he was obliged to leave in the village, while he ascended the mountain.

At the cool and fresh hour of day-break he assembled his scanty band, and began to climb the height, wishing to reach the top before the heat of noon.

About ten o'clock they came out from the thick forest through which they had been struggling ever since day-break: the change from the closeness of the woods to the pleasant breeze from the mountain, was delightful. But they were still further encouraged. "From that spot" exclaimed one of the Indian guides, pointing to the height above them "may be seen the great sea of which you are in search."

When Balboa heard this, he commanded his men to halt, and forbade any one to stir from his place. He was resolved to be the first European who should look upon that sea, which he had been the first to discover.

Accordingly he ascended the mountain height alone, and when he reached the summit he beheld the wide sea glittering in the morning sun.

Balboa called to his little troop to ascend the height and look upon the glorious prospect; and they joined him without delay.

"Behold, my friends," said he, "the reward of all our toils, a sight upon which the eye of Spaniard never rested before."

He now took possession of the sea-coast and the surrounding country in the name of the king of Spain.

He then had a tree cut down, and made into the form of a cross, and planted it on the spot from which he had first beheld the sea. He also made a mound by heaping up large stones upon which he carved the names of the king of Spain.

The Indians saw all this done, and while they helped to pile the stones and set up the cross, they little thought that they were assisting to deprive themselves of their homes and their country.

You remember the noble reproof of Canute in the "History of England," to his flatterers, when they assured him that even the waves of the sea would obey him: but this arrogant and weak minded Spaniard waded into the waves of the great Pacific Ocean, up to his knees, and absurdly took possession of it in the name of the Spanish monarch.

Balboa was some time employed in fighting with the Indian tribes that inhabited the sea-coast, and in hunting them with blood-hounds.

He soon made these helpless people submit. From them he got some further accounts of the rich country which the Indian prince had mentioned, and which proved afterwards to be Peru.

He now quitted the shores of the Pacific Ocean on his return across the mountains of Darien. His route homewards was different from that which he had before pursued, and the sufferings of his troops much greater.

Often they could find no water, the heat having dried up the pools and brooks. Many died from thirst, and those who survived, although loaded with gold, were exhausted for want of food; for the poor Indians brought gold and jewels, instead of food, as peace offerings to the Spaniards.

At length, after much slaughter of the Indians that dwelt in the mountains, and burning of the villages, Balboa and his troops arrived at Darien; having robbed the Indians of all the gold and silver they could find. The Spaniards at Darien received with great delight and praise the news of his success and discovery—a discovery gained at the expense of much unnecessary cruelty and injustice.

He now despatched a ship to Spain, with the news of his discovery, and by it he sent part of the gold he had carried off from the different Indian tribes.

A few days before this ship reached Spain a new governor had been sent out, by name Padrarias Davila, to take Balboa's place, and with orders to punish Balboa for his conduct to Enciso.

But when he arrived at Darien, and saw how much the discoverer of the Pacific was beloved by all the Spaniards of the settlement he hesitated through fear, and finally resolved to defer the execution of the orders which he had brought with him.

Davila permitted Balboa to depart from Darien for the purpose of building brigantines with a view to navigate and explore the Pacific Ocean. Three years had elapsed since he discovered this ocean, and with joy he now prepared to build the ships which were to be the first belonging to Europeans to sail upon it.

Balboa having overcome all his difficulties, had the satisfaction of seeing two brigantines finished and floating on a river which they called the Balsas.

As soon as they had been made ready for sea, he embarked with some of his followers, and sailing down the river, was the first to launch into the ocean that he had been the first to discover. But his death was now about to put a stop to his further discoveries.

The new governor, Davila, who was a bad and cruel man, and envious of Balboa, on account of the discoveries he had made, had long resolved to put him to death.

The time having, as he thought, arrived, which was favourable for his villanous design, he sent for Balboa to return, and on his arrival he had him seized by one of his early friends and followers, Franciso Pizarro, and then, after throwing him into prison, he ordered him to be put to death by having his head cut off.

This unjust sentence was executed, and Balboa, after a mock trial, was publicly beheaded, in the 48th year of his age.

CHAPTER X.

PARLEY TELLS OF THE CONQUEST OF MEXICO.

Not long after this another expedition sailed from Cuba, under the command of Cordova, to make further discoveries on the new continent.

The first land they saw proved to be the eastern cape of that large peninsula which you see in the map projecting into the gulf of Mexico, and which still retains its original name of Yucatan.

As they approached the shore, five canoes came off full of people decently clad in cotton garments; this excited the wonder of the Spaniards, who had found every other part they had yet visited, possessed by naked savages.

Cordova endeavoured to gain their good-will by presents, but perceived they were preparing to attack him; and, as his water began to fail, he sailed further along the coast in hopes of procuring a supply, but not a single river did he find all along that coast till he came to Potonchon, in the bay of Campeachy, which is on the western side of the peninsula.

Here Cordova landed all his troops, in order to protect the sailors while filling their casks; but, notwithstanding, the natives rushed down upon them with such fury and in such numbers, that forty-seven of the Spaniards were killed upon the spot, and one man only of the whole body escaped unhurt.

Cordova, though wounded in twelve places, led off his wounded men with great presence of mind and fortitude, and with much difficulty they reached their ships, and hastened back to Cuba. Cordova died of his wounds soon after his arrival.

Notwithstanding the ill success of this expedition, another was shortly after fitted out under the command of Grijalva, a young man of known merit and courage. He directed his course to the bay of Campeachy, to the part from which Cordova had returned, and as they advanced they saw many villages scattered along the coast, in which they could distinguish houses of stone that appeared white and lofty at a distance.

In the warmth of their admiration, they fancied these to be cities, adorned with towers and pinnacles; and one of the soldiers happening to remark that this country resembled Spain in appearance, Grijalva, with universal applause, called it New Spain; the name which still distinguishes this extensive and opulent province of the Spanish dominions.

They landed to the west of Tabasco, where they were received with the respect due to superior beings; the people perfumed them as they landed with incense of gum copal, and presented to them offerings of the choicest delicacies of their country.

They were extremely fond of trading with their new visitants, and in six days, the Spaniards obtained ornaments of gold, and of curious workmanship, to the amount of fifteen thousand pesoes, an immense sum, in exchange for European toys of small price.

They learned from the natives that they were the subjects of a great monarch, whose dominions extended over that and many other provinces.

Grijalva now returned with a full account of the important discoveries he had made, and with all the treasure he had acquired by trafficking with the natives.

The favourable account of New Spain brought by Grijalva, determined Velasquez, the governor of Cuba, seriously to undertake the conquest of that country, but as he did not wish to take the command himself, he endeavoured to find a person who would act under his directions.

After much deliberation he fixed upon Fernando Cortez, a man of restless and ardent spirit, on whom he had conferred many benefits; but these Cortez soon forgot, and was no sooner invested with the command than he threw off the authority of Velasquez altogether.

The greatest force that could be collected for the conquest of a great empire, amounted to no more than five hundred and eight men, only thirteen of whom were armed with muskets; thirty-two were cross-bowmen, and the rest had swords and spears; they had only sixteen horses, and ten small field-pieces.

With such a slender and ill provided force did Cortez set sail to make war upon a monarch whose dominions were more extensive than all the kingdoms subject to the Spanish crown.

On his voyage Cortez first landed on the island of Cozumel, where he redeemed from slavery Jerome de Aguilar, a Spaniard, who had been eight years a prisoner among the Indians, and having learned the Yucatan language (which is spoken in all those parts), proved afterwards extremely useful as an interpreter.

He then proceeded to the river of Tabasco, where the disposition of the natives proved very hostile, and they showed the most determined resistance; but the noise of the artillery, the appearances of the floating fortresses which brought the Spaniards over the ocean, and the horses on which they fought, all new objects to the natives, inspired them with astonishment mingled with terror; they regarded the Spaniards as gods, and sent them supplies of provisions, with a present of some gold and twenty female slaves.

Cortez here learned that the native sovereign, who was called Montezuma, reigned over an extensive empire, and that thirty vassals, called caziques, obeyed him; that his riches were immense, and his power absolute. No more was necessary to inflame the ambition of Cortez, and the avarice of his followers.

He then proceeded along the coast till he came to St. Juan de Ulua, where, having laid the foundation of Vera Cruz, he caused himself to be elected Captain-general of the new colony.

Here he was visited by two native caziques, whose names were Teutile and Pilpatoe, who entered his camp with a numerous retinue, and informed him that they were persons entrusted with the government of that province by a great monarch, whom they called Montezuma, and that they were sent to inquire what his intentions were in visiting their coast, and to offer him what assistance he might need.

Cortez received them with much formal ceremony, and informed them that he came from Don Carlos of Austria, the greatest monarch of all the east, with propositions of such moment, that he could impart them to none but the emperor himself; and requested them to conduct him, without loss of time, into the presence of their master.

Messengers were immediately despatched to Montezuma, with a full account of everything that had passed.

The Mexican monarch, in order to obtain early information, had couriers posted along the road, and the intelligence was conveyed by a very curious contrivance called picture writing, persons being employed to represent, in a series of pictures, everything that passed, which was the Mexican mode of writing: Teutile and Pilpatoe were employed to deliver the answer of their master, but as they knew how repugnant it was to the wishes and schemes of the Spanish commander, they would not make it known till they had first endeavoured to soothe and pacify him. For this purpose they introduced a train of a hundred Indians loaded with presents sent to him by Montezuma.

The magnificence of these far exceeded any idea which the Spaniards had formed of his wealth.

They were placed on mats spread on the ground, in such order as showed them to the greatest advantage. Cortez and his officers viewed with admiration the various manufactures of the country. Cotton stuffs so fine as to resemble silk. Pictures of animals, trees, and other natural objects, formed with feathers of different colours, disposed with such skill and elegance, as to resemble, in truth and beauty of imitation, the finest paintings. But what chiefly attracted their eyes were two large plates of circular form; one of massive gold, representing the sun, the other of silver, an emblem of the moon. These were accompanied with bracelets, collars, rings, and other trinkets of gold, and with several boxes filled with pearls, precious stones, and grains of gold unwrought, as they had been found in the mines or rivers.

Cortez received all these with an appearance of profound respect for the monarch by whom they were bestowed; but when the Mexican informed him that their master would not give his consent that foreign troops should approach nearer to his capital, or even allow them to continue longer in his dominions, the Spanish general declared that he must insist on his first demand, as he could not, without dishonour, return to his own country until he was admitted into the presence of the princes whom he was appointed by his sovereign to visit.

He first caused all his vessels to be burnt, in order to cut off the possibility of retreat, and to show his soldiers that they must either conquer or perish. He then penetrated into the interior of the country, drew to his camp several caziques, hostile to Montezuma, and induced these native princes to assist him.

After surmounting every obstacle he arrived with his army in sight of the immense lake on which was built the city of Mexico, the capital of the empire.

In descending from the mountains of Chalco, the vast plain of Mexico opened gradually to their view, displaying a prospect the most striking and beautiful: fertile and cultivated fields, stretched out further than the eye could reach, a lake resembling the sea in extent, encompassed with large towns, and the capital city rising upon an island, adorned with temples and turrets.

Many messengers arrived one after another from Montezuma, one day permitting them to advance, on the next requiring them to retire, as his hopes or fears alternately prevailed, and so wonderful was his infatuation that Cortez was almost at the gates of the capital before the monarch had determined whether to receive him as a friend or oppose him as an enemy, but as no signs of hostility appeared, the Spaniards continued their march along the causeway which led to Mexico through the lake with great circumspection, though without seeming to suspect the prince whom they were about to visit.

When they drew near the city, about a thousand persons who appeared to be of distinction, came out to meet them, adorned with plumes and clad in mantles of fine cotton.

Each of these as they passed Cortez, saluted him according to the mode of their country; they announced the approach of Montezuma himself, and soon his harbingers came in sight.

There appeared first two hundred persons in uniform dresses, with large plumes of feathers, marching two and two in deep silence, barefooted, with their eyes fixed on the ground.

Then followed a company of higher rank, in their most shewy apparel. In the midst of these was Montezuma, in a chair or litter, richly ornamented with gold and feathers of various colours. Four of his principal favourites carried him on their shoulders; others supported a canopy of curious workmanship over his head: before him marched three officers with rods of gold in their hands, which they lifted on high at certain intervals.

At that signal all the people bowed their heads and hid their faces, as unworthy to look on so great a monarch.

When he drew near, Cortez dismounted advancing towards him in respectful posture; at the same time Montezuma alighted from his chair, and leaning on the arm of two of his nearest relations, approached him with a slow and stately pace, his attendants covering the way with cotton cloths, that he might not touch the ground.

Cortez accosted him with profound reverence, after the European fashion. He returned the salutation, according to the mode of his country, by touching the earth with his hand and then kissing it.

This condescension, in so proud a monarch, made all his subjects believe that the Spaniards were something more than human.

Montezuma conducted Cortez to the quarters which he had ordered for his reception, and immediately took his leave, with a politeness not unworthy of a court more refined.

"You are now," said he, "with your brothers, in your own house: refresh yourselves after your fatigue, and be happy until I return."

The place allotted for the Spaniards was a magnificent palace built by the father of Montezuma. It was surrounded by a stone wall with towers, and its apartments and courts were so large as to accommodate both the Spaniards and their Indian allies.

The first care of Cortez was to take precautions for his security, by planting artillery so as to command the different avenues which led to it, and posting sentinels at proper stations, with orders to observe the greatest vigilance.

In the evening Montezuma returned to visit his guests, with the same pomp as in their first interview, and brought presents of great value not only to Cortez and his officers, but even to the private men. A long conference ensued, in which Cortez, in his usual style, magnified the power and dignity of his sovereign.

Next morning Cortez and some of his principal attendants were admitted to a public audience of the emperor; the three following days were employed in viewing the city, the appearance of which was so far superior to any place the Spaniards had beheld in America, and yet so little resembling the structure of an European city, that it filled them with surprise and admiration.

Mexico, or Tenuchtitlan, as it was anciently called, is situated on some small islands, near one side of a large lake, which is ninety miles in circumference. The access to the city was by artificial causeways or streets, formed of stones and earth, about thirty feet in breadth. These causeways were of considerable length: that on the west extended a mile and a half; that on the north-west three miles, and that towards the south six miles. On the east, the city could only be approached by canoes.

Not only the temples of their Gods, but the palaces belonging to the monarch, and to persons of distinction, were of such dimensions that they might be termed magnificent.

But, however the Spaniards might be amused or astonished at these objects, they felt the utmost anxiety with respect to their situation.

They had been allowed to penetrate into the heart of a powerful kingdom, and were now lodged in its capital without having once met with open opposition from its monarch; but they had pushed forward into a situation where it was difficult to continue, and from which it was impossible to retire without disgrace and ruin.

They could not, however, doubt of the hostility of the Mexicans, more especially as, on his march, Cortez received advice from Vera Cruz, where he had left a garrison, that a Mexican general had marched to attack the rebels whom the Spaniards had encouraged to revolt against Montezuma, and that the commander of the garrison had marched out with some of his troops to support the rebels, that an engagement had ensued, in which, though the Spaniards were victorious, the Spanish general with seven of his men, had been mortally wounded, his horse killed, and one Spaniard taken alive, and that the head of his unfortunate captive had been sent to Mexico, after being carried in triumph to different cities in order to convince the people that their invaders were not immortal.

In this trying situation, he fixed upon a plan no less extraordinary than daring; he determined to seize Montezuma in his palace and to carry him a prisoner to the Spanish quarters. This he immediately proposed to his officers, who, as it was the only resource in which there appeared any safety, warmly approved of it, and it was agreed instantly to make the attempt.

At his usual hour of visiting Montezuma, Cortez went to the palace, accompanied by five of his principal officers, and as many trusty soldiers; thirty chosen men followed, not in regular order, but sauntering at some distance, as if they had no object but curiosity: the remainder of his troops continued under arms, ready to sally out on the first alarm.

Cortez and his attendants were admitted without suspicion, the Mexicans retiring, as usual, out of respect.

He now addressed the monarch in a tone very different from that which he had employed on former occasions, and a conversation ensued, very much resembling that between the wolf and the lamb, in the fable, which you no doubt remember.

Cortez bitterly reproached him as the author of the violent assault made by the Mexican general upon the Spaniards, and with having caused the death of some of his companions.

Montezuma, with great earnestness, asserted his innocence, but Cortez affected not to believe him, and proposed that, as a proof of his sincerity, he should remove from his own palace, and take up his residence in the Spanish quarters.

The first mention of so strange a proposal almost bereaved Montezuma of speech; at length he haughtily answered "That persons of his rank were not accustomed voluntarily to give themselves up as prisoners, and were he mean enough to do so, his subjects would not permit such an affront to be offered to their sovereign."

Cortez now endeavoured to soothe, and then to intimidate him, and in this way the altercation continued three hours, when Velasquez de Leon, an impetuous young man exclaimed, "Why waste more time in vain? Let us seize him instantly, or stab him to the heart." The threatening voice and fierce gesture with which these words were uttered, struck Montezuma with a sense of his danger, and abandoning himself to his fate, he complied with their request: his officers were called, he communicated to them his resolution. Though astonished and affected, they presumed not to question the will of their master, but carried him in silent pomp, all bathed in tears, to the Spanish quarters.

Cortez at first pretended to treat Montezuma with great respect, but soon took care to let him know that he was entirely in his power. Being thus master of the person of the monarch, he demanded that the Mexican general who had attacked the Spaniards, his son, and five of the principal officers who served under him, should be brought prisoners to Mexico, and delivered into his hands.

As Cortez wished that the shedding the blood of a Spaniard should appear the most heinous crime that could be committed, he then ordered these brave men, who had only acted as became loyal subjects in opposing the invaders of their country, to be burnt alive, before the gates of the imperial palace.

The unhappy victims were led forth, and laid on a pile composed of the weapons collected in the royal magazine for the public defence.

During this cruel execution, Cortez entered the apartments of Montezuma, and caused him to be loaded with irons, in order to force him to acknowledge himself a vassal of the king of Spain. The unhappy prince yielded, and was restored to a semblance of liberty on presenting the fierce conqueror with six hundred thousand marks of pure gold, and a prodigious quantity of precious stones.

The Mexicans driven to desperation, all at once flew to arms, and made so sudden and violent an attack that all the valour and skill of Cortez was scarcely sufficient to repel them.

The Spaniards now found themselves enclosed in a hostile city, the whole population of which was exasperated to the highest pitch against them, and without some extraordinary exertion they were inevitably undone. Cortez therefore made a desperate sally, but after exerting his utmost efforts for a whole day, was obliged to retreat to his quarters with the loss of twelve men killed, and upwards of sixty wounded; Cortez himself was wounded in the hand.

The Spanish general now betook himself to the only resource which was left, namely, to try what effect the interposition of Montezuma would have to soothe and overawe his subjects.

When the Mexicans approached next morning to renew the assault, that unfortunate prince, who was now reduced to the sad necessity of becoming the instrument of his own disgrace, and of the slavery of his people, advanced to the battlements in his royal robes, and with all the pomp in which he used to appear on solemn occasions. At the sight of their sovereign, whom they had long been accustomed to reverence almost as a god, the Mexicans instantly forebore their hostilities; and many prostrated themselves on the ground; but when he addressed them in favour of the Spaniards, and made use of all the arguments he could think of to mitigate their rage, they testified their resentment with loud murmurings, and at length broke forth with such fury, that before the soldiers appointed to guard Montezuma had time to cover him with their shields, he was wounded with two arrows and a blow on the temple with a stone struck him to the ground.

On seeing him fall, the Mexicans instantly fled with the utmost precipitation, and Montezuma was conveyed to his apartments, whither Cortez followed in order to console him; but as the unhappy monarch now perceived that he was become an object of contempt even to his own subjects, his haughty spirit revived, and scorning to prolong his life after this last humiliation, he tore the bandages from his wounds, in a transport of rage, and refusing to take any nourishment, he soon ended his wretched days; refusing with disdain all the solicitations of the Spaniards to embrace the Christian faith.

The Mexicans having chosen his son Guatimozin emperor, attacked the head quarters of Cortez with the utmost fury, and, in spite of the advantages of fire-arms, forced the Spaniards to retire, which alone saved them from destruction. Their rear guard was cut to pieces, and suffered severely during the retreat, which lasted six days.

The Spaniards, however, having received fresh troops from Spain, defeated the Mexicans, and took Guatimozin prisoner, and in the end succeeded in totally subjugating this vast empire.

Guatimozin, before he was taken prisoner, being aware of his impending fate, had ordered all his treasures to be thrown into the lake, and he was now put to the torture, on suspicion of having concealed his treasure. This was done by laying him on burning coals; but he bore whatever the cruelty of his tormentors could inflict, with the invincible fortitude of an American warrior. One of his chief favourites, his fellow sufferer, being overcome by the violence of the anguish, turned a dejected eye towards his master, which seemed to implore his permission to reveal all he knew. But the high spirited prince darted on him a look of authority mingled with scorn, and checked his weakness by asking, "Am I reposing on a bed of flowers?"

Overawed by the reproach, he persevered in dutiful silence and expired.

Cortes, utterly regardless of what crimes and cruelties he committed, added largely to the Spanish territory and revenue. But Spain was always ungrateful. Pizarro was murdered; Columbus died of a broken heart, and Balboa the death of a felon; so what could Cortez expect? He fell into neglect and poverty when his work was done. One day he forced his way through the crowd that had collected about the carriage of the sovereign, mounted the door-step, and looked in. Astonished at so gross a breach of etiquette, the monarch demanded to know who he was? "I am a man," replied Cortez, "who has given you more provinces than your ancestors left you cities!"

CHAPTER XI.

PARLEY RELATES HOW PIZARRO DISCOVERED AND CONQUERED PERU.

Peru, when first discovered by the Spaniards, was a large and flourishing empire, including two kingdoms, Peru, and Quito, and extended over nearly half of the widest part of the South American Continent, as you will see if you look into the map, Brazil occupying the other half of the wide part.

It had been governed by a long succession of Emperors, who were called the Incas of Peru.

On the 14th of Nov. 1524, three Spanish adventurers whose names were Francisco

Pizarro, in early life a feeder of swine, Diego de Almagro, and Hernando Luque, set sail from Panama for the discovery of Peru.

Panama was a new settlement which the Spaniards had formed on the western side of the Isthmus of Darien, on the shores of the Pacific Ocean.

Pizarro had only a single ship and one hundred and twenty men, to undertake this discovery, and so little was he acquainted with the climate of America, that the most improper season of the whole year was chosen for his departure; the periodical winds which were then set in, being directly opposite to the course he proposed to steer.

He spent two years in sailing from Panama to the northern extremity of Peru, a voyage which is now frequently performed in a fortnight.

At Tumbez, a place about three degrees south of the line, Pizarro and his companions feasted their eyes with the first view of the opulence and civilization of the Peruvian empire.

This place was distinguished for its stately temple, and for one of the palaces of the Incas, or sovereigns of the country.

But what chiefly attracted their notice, was such a show of gold and silver, not only in the ornaments of their persons and temples, but in the several vessels and utensils of common use, as left them no room to doubt that these metals abounded in the greatest profusion.

Having explored the country sufficiently to satisfy his own mind, Pizarro hastened back to Panama, and from thence to Spain, where he obtained from Charles the Fifth the most liberal concessions, himself being made chief governor of all the countries he should subdue; Almagro, king's lieutenant, and Luque being appointed first bishop of Peru.

Thus encouraged, Pizarro returned to Panama, whence he soon after sailed with three small vessels, containing only one hundred and eighty-six soldiers, and arrived at the Bay of St. Matthew; he then advanced by land as quickly as possible towards Peru.

When Pizarro landed in the bay of St. Matthew, a civil war was raging with the greatest fury between Atahualpa, who was then seated on the throne of Peru, and his brother.

This contest so much engaged the attention of the Peruvians, that they never once attempted to check the progress of the Spaniards, and Pizarro determined to take advantage of these dissensions.

He directed his course towards Caxamalia, a small town at the distance of twelve days' march from St. Michael, where Atahualpa was encamped with a considerable body of troops.

Before he had proceeded far, an officer, despatched by the Inca, met him with valuable presents from that prince, accompanied with a proffer of his alliance, and his assurance of a friendly reception at Caxamalia.

Pizarro, according to the usual artifice of his countrymen, pretended to come as the ambassador of a powerful monarch, to offer his aid against those enemies who disputed his title to the throne.

The Peruvians were altogether unable to comprehend the object of the Spaniards in entering their country, whether they should consider them as beings of a superior nature, who had visited them from some beneficent motive, as the Spaniards wished them to believe, or whether they were sent as evil demons to punish them for their crimes, as the rapaciousness and cruelty of the Spaniards led them to apprehend.

Pizarro's declaration of his pacific intentions, however, so far removed all the Inca's fears, that he determined to give him a friendly reception.

In consequence of this the Spaniards were allowed to march across a sandy desert, which lay in their way to Metupe, where the smallest efforts of an opposing enemy might have proved fatal to them, and then through a defile so narrow, that a few men might have defended it against a numerous army; but here, likewise, they met with no opposition.

Pizarro, having reached Caxamalia with his followers, sent messengers, inviting Atahualpa to visit him in his quarters, which he readily promised. On the return of these messengers, they gave such a description of the wealth which they had seen, as determined Pizarro to seize upon the Peruvian monarch, in order that he might more easily come at the riches of his kingdom.

The next day the Inca approached Caxamalia, without suspicion of Pizarro's treachery; but, as he drew near the Spanish quarters, Vincent Valverde, chaplain to the expedition, advanced with a crucifix in one hand and a breviary in the other, and, in a long discourse, attempted to convert him to the Roman Catholic faith.

This the monarch declined, avowing his resolution to adhere to the worship of the sun; at the same time wished to know where the priest had learned these extraordinary things he had related. "In this book!" answered Valverde, reaching out his breviary.

The Inca opened it eagerly, and turning over the leaves, raised it to his ear, "This," said he, "is silent, it tells me nothing;" and threw it with disdain to the ground.

The enraged monk, running towards his countrymen, cried out, "To arms, Christians! to arms! the word of God is insulted—avenge the profanation of these impious dogs!"

Pizarro immediately gave the signal of assault, which ended in the destruction of four thousand Peruvians, without the loss of a single Spaniard. The plunder was rich beyond any idea which even the conquerors had yet formed concerning the wealth of Peru. The Inca, who was taken prisoner, quickly discovered that the ruling passion of the Spaniards was the desire of gold; he offered therefore to recover his liberty by a splendid ransom.

The apartment in which he was confined was twenty-two feet long, by sixteen in breadth; this he undertook to fill with vessels of gold as high as he could reach.

Pizarro closed with the proposal, and a line was drawn upon the walls of the chamber, to mark the stipulated height to which the treasure was to rise.

During this confinement, Atahualpa had attached himself with peculiar affection to Ferdinand Pizarro, and Hernando Soto; who, as they were persons of birth and education, superior to the rough adventurers with whom they served, were accustomed to behave with more decency and kindness to the captive monarch.

Soothed with this respect, he delighted in their society; but in the presence of the governor he was always uneasy and overawed, and this dread soon became mingled with contempt.

Among all the European arts, what he admired most was that of reading and writing, and he long deliberated with himself whether it was a natural or an acquired talent. In order to determine this, he desired one of the soldiers, who guarded him, to write the name of God on the nail of his thumb. This he showed successively to several Spaniards, asking its meaning, and to his amazement, they all, without hesitation returned the same answer. At length Francisco Pizarro entered, and on presenting it to him, he blushed, and with some confusion was obliged to acknowledge that he could not read.

From that moment Atahualpa considered him as a mean person, less instructed than his own soldiers, nor could he conceal the sentiments of contempt with which this discovery inspired him. He, however, performed his part of the contract, and the gold which his subjects brought in, was worth three or four hundred thousand pounds sterling.

When they assembled to divide the spoils of this innocent people, procured by deceit, extortion, and cruelty, the transaction began with a solemn invocation to Heaven, as if they expected the guidance of God in distributing the wages of iniquity. In this division, eight thousand pesoes, at that time equal in value to £10,000 sterling, of the present day, fell to the share of each soldier: Pizarro and his officers received shares in proportion to the dignity of their rank.

The Spaniards having divided the treasure among them, the Inca insisted that they should fulfil their promise of setting him at liberty. But the Spaniards, with unparalleled treachery and cruelty had now determined to put him to death; an action the most criminal and atrocious that stains the Spanish name, amidst all the deeds of violence committed in carrying on the conquest of the New World. In order to give some colour of justice to this outrage, Pizarro resolved to try the Inca, according to the forms of the criminal courts of Spain, and having constituted himself chief judge, charges the most absurd, and even ridiculous, were brought against him; but, as his infamous judges had predetermined, he was found guilty, and condemned to be burnt alive.

Atahualpa, astonished at his fate, endeavoured to avert it by tears, by promises, and by entreaties; but pity never touched the unfeeling heart of Pizarro. He ordered him to be led instantly to execution, and the cruel priest, after having prostituted his sacred office to confirm the wicked sentence, offered to console, and attempted to convert him.

The dread of a cruel death, extorted from the trembling victim his consent to be baptized. The ceremony was performed; and Atahualpa, instead of being burnt alive, was strangled at the stake.

Pizarro then proceeded in his career of cruelty and rapacity, till, in ten years, he subdued the whole of this great empire, and divided it among his followers.

In making the division, he allotted the richest and finest provinces to himself and his favourites, giving the less valuable to Almagro and his friends.

This partiality highly offended Almagro, who thought his claims equal to Pizarro's, and this led to open hostilities; when Almagro being taken prisoner, he was beheaded in prison by order of Pizarro.

Soon after this, Pizarro himself was assassinated in his palace by a party of Almagro's friends, headed by the son of Almagro, in revenge for the death of his father.

Some time before this, the cruel and bigoted priest, Val de Viridi, had been beaten to death with the butt end of muskets, in the island of Puma, at the instigation of Almagro.

Thus retributive justice, in the end, overtook these unjust and cruel men.

CHAPTER XII.

PARLEY DESCRIBES THE NATURAL BEAUTIES OF AMERICA.

Let us now leave for a while the cruel Spaniards, and talk about the beauties of nature, in these new discovered countries.

In these extensive regions, every thing appeared new and wonderful; not only the inhabitants, but the whole face of nature was totally different from anything that had been seen in Europe.

Grand ridges of mountains, numerous volcanoes, some of them, though under the Equator, covered with perpetual snows. Noble rivers, whose course, in several instances, exceeds three thousand miles.

Here are found the palm-tree, the cedar, the tamarind, the guaiacum, the sassafras, the hickory, the chestnut, the walnut of many different kinds, the wild cherry (sometimes a hundred feet high), and more than fifty different sorts of oak.

The plane, of which there are two kinds, one found in Asia, which is called the oriental plane: that found in America is called the occidental plane; but the Americans call it button-wood, or sycamore. Its foliage is richer, and its leaves of a more beautiful green than the oriental. It grows to a great size.

The cypress is perhaps the largest of the American trees; it is a more than a hundred and twenty feet high; and the diameter of the trunk at forty or fifty feet from the ground is sometimes eight or ten feet.

Another tree of gigantic magnitude is the wild cotton or Cuba tree. A canoe made from the single trunk of this tree has been know to contain a hundred persons.

Above all these in beauty is the majestic magnolia which shoots up to the height of more than a hundred feet; its trunk perfectly straight, surmounted by a thick expanded head of pale green foliage, in the form of a cone.

From the centre of the flowery crown which terminates each of its branches, a flower of the purest white arises, having the form of a rose, from six to nine inches in diameter.

To the flower succeeds a crimson cone; this, in opening, exhibits round seeds of the finest coral red, surrounded by delicate threads, six inches long.

Here, every plant and tree displays its most majestic form.

Upon the shady banks of the Madelina there grows a climbing plant which the botanists call Aristolochia, the flowers of which are four feet in circumference, and children amuse themselves with covering their heads with them as hats.

The Banana which grows in all the hot parts of America, and furnishes the Indians with the chief part of their daily food, producing more nutritious substance, in less space, and with less trouble than any other known plant.

It is here that the ground produces the sugar-cane, the coffee, and the cocoa-nut from which is produced the chocolate. The vanilla, the anana or pine apple, and many other delicious fruits.

The cacao, though generally pronounced cocoa, must not be confounded with the Cocoa Palm which produces that largest of all nuts, the Cocoa-nut.

These trees and plants which I have mentioned, and many more equally beautiful, are all natives of the American woods.

But the European settlers, when they came, brought over to Europe many valuable kinds of fruit and plants, which they did not find here; and I never was more delighted than once on passing through Virginia, to observe the dwellings of the settlers shaded by orange, lemon, and pomegranate trees, that fill the air with the perfume of their flowers, while their branches are loaded with fruit.

Strawberries of native growth, of the richest flavour, spring up beneath your feet; and when these are passed away, every grove and field looks like a cherry orchard. Then follow the peaches, every hedge-row is planted with them. But it is the flowers and the flowering shrubs, that, beyond all else, render these regions so beautiful. No description can give an idea of the variety, the profusion, and the luxuriance of them.

The Dog-wood, whose lateral fan-like branches are dotted all over with star-like blossoms of splendid white, as large as those of the gumcistus.

The straight silvery column of the Papan fig, crowned with a canopy of large indented leaves; and the wild orange tree, mixed with the odoriferous and common laurel, form striking ornaments of this enchanting scene, with many other lovely flowers too numerous to describe.

There is another charm that enchants the wanderer in the American woods. In a bright day in the summer months you walk through an atmosphere of butterflies, so gaudy in hue, and so varied in form, that I often thought they looked like flowers on the wing.

Some of them are large, measuring three or four inches across the wing, but many, and those of the most beautiful, are small. Some have wings the most dainty lavender, and bodies of black; others are fawn and rose colour, and others are orange and bright blue: but pretty as they are, it is their numbers more than their beauty; and their gay, and noiseless movement through the air, crossing each other in chequered maze, that so delights the eye.

That beautiful production, the humming bird, is also the sportive inhabitant of these warm climates, and I think they surpass all the works of nature in singularity of form, splendour of colour, and variety of species.

They are found in all the West India islands and in most parts of the American continent: the smallest species does not exceed the size of some of the bees.

There are so many different kinds, and each so beautiful, that it is impossible to describe them. They are constantly on the wing, collecting insects from the blossoms of the tamarind, the orange, or any other tree that happens to be in flower: and the humming noise proceeds from the surprising velocity with which they move their wings.

CHAPTER XIII.

PARLEY TELLS OF THE FIRST ENGLISH COLONY IN AMERICA.

In the beginning of the reign of James the First, who you know succeeded Elizabeth, the first successful attempt was made by the English to found a colony in America.

Three small vessels, of which the largest did not exceed one hundred tons burden, under the command of Captain Newport, formed the first squadron that was to execute what had been so long, and so vainly attempted; and sailed with a hundred and five men destined to remain in America.

Several of these emigrants were members of distinguished families—particularly George Percy, a brother of the Earl of Northumberland; and several were officers of reputation, of whom we may notice Bartholomew Gosnald, the navigator, and Captain John Smith, one of the most distinguished ornaments of an age that abounded with memorable men.

Thus, after the lapse of a hundred and ten years from the discovery of the continent by

Cabot, and twenty-two years after its first occupation by Raleigh, was the number of the English colonists limited to a hundred and five; and this handful of men undertook the arduous task of peopling a remote and uncultivated land, covered with woods and marshes, and inhabited only by savages and beasts of prey.

Newport and his squadron did not accomplish their voyage in less than four months; but its termination was rendered particularly fortunate by the effect of a storm, which defeated their purpose of landing and settling at Roanoak, and carried them into the bay of Chesapeak; and coasting along its southern shore, they entered a river which the natives called Powhatan, and explored its banks for more than forty miles from its mouth.

The adventurers, impressed with the superior advantages of the coast and region to which they had been thus happily conducted, determined to make this the place of their abode.

They gave to their infant settlement, as well as to the neighbouring river, the name of their king; and James Town retains the distinction of being the oldest of existing habitations of the English in America.

Newport having landed the colonists, with what supplies of provisions were destined for their support, set sail with his ships to return to England, in the month of June, 1607.

The colonists soon found themselves limited to a scanty supply of unwholesome provisions; and the heat and moisture of the climate combining with the effect of their diet, brought on diseases that raged with fatal violence.

Before the month of September, one half of their number had miserably perished, and among these victims was Bartholomew Gosnald, who had planned the expedition, and greatly contributed to its success.

This scene of suffering was embittered by dissensions among themselves. At length, in the extremity of their distress, when ruin seemed to threaten them, as well from famine as the fury of the savages, the colonists obtained a complete and unexpected deliverance, which the piety of Smith ascribed to the influence of God in their behalf.

The savages, actuated by a sudden change of feeling, not only refrained from molesting them, but brought them, without being asked, a supply of provisions so liberal, as at once to remove their apprehensions of famine and hostility.

The colonists were now instructed by their misfortunes, and the sense of urgent danger, led them to submit to the advice of the man, whose talents were most likely to extricate them from the difficulties with which they were surrounded.

Every eye was now turned on Captain Smith, whose superior talents and experience, had so far excited the envy and jealousy of his colleagues, that he had been excluded from a seat in the council.

Under Captain Smith's directions, James Town was fortified, so as to repel the attacks of the savages, and its inhabitants were provided with dwellings that afforded shelter from the weather, and contributed to restore and preserve their health.

Finding the supplies of the savages discontinued, he took with him some of his people and penetrated into the interior of the country, where by courtesy and kindness to the tribes whom he found well disposed, he succeeded in procuring a plentiful supply of provisions. In the midst of his successes he was surprised during an expedition by a hostile body of savages, who having made him prisoner, after a gallant and nearly successful defence, prepared to inflict on him the usual fate of their captives.

His genius and presence of mind did not desert him on this trying occasion. He desired to speak with the sachem or chief of the tribe to which he was a prisoner, and, presenting him with a mariner's compass, expatiated on the wonderful discoveries to which this little instrument had led, described the shape of the earth, the vastness of its land and oceans, the course of the sun and the varieties of nations, wisely forbearing to express any solicitude for his life.

The savages listened to him with amazement and admiration. They handled the compass, viewing with surprise the play of the needle, which they plainly saw, but were unable to touch; and he appeared to have gained some ascendancy over their minds.

For an hour afterwards they seemed undecided; but their habitual disposition returning, they bound him to a tree, and were preparing to despatch him with their arrows.

But a deeper impression had been made by his harangue on the mind of their chief, who, holding up the compass in his hand, gave the signal of reprieve, and Smith, though still guarded as a prisoner, was conducted to a dwelling, where he was kindly treated and plentifully entertained.

But after vainly attempting to prevail on their captive to betray the English colony into their hands, the Indian referred his fate to Powhatan, the king or principal sachem of the country, to whose presence they conducted him in pompous and triumphant procession.

This prince received him with much ceremony, ordered a rich repast to be set before him, and then adjudged him to suffer death by having his head laid on a stone and beaten to pieces with clubs.

At the place appointed for his execution, Smith was again rescued from impending destruction by Pocahontas, the favourite daughter of the chief, who, finding her first entreaties disregarded, threw her arms round the prisoner, and declared her determination to save him or die with him.

Her generous compassion prevailed over the cruelty of her tribe, and the king not only gave Smith his life, but soon after sent him back to James Town, where the benificence of Pocahontas continued to follow him with supplies of provisions that delivered the colony from famine.

This eminent commander continued for some time to govern the colony with the greatest wisdom and prudence, when he received a dangerous wound from the accidental explosion of some gunpowder. Completely disabled by this misfortune, and destitute of surgical aid in the colony, he was compelled to resign his command, and take his departure for England. He never returned to Virginia again.

CHAPTER XIV.

PARLEY TELLS OF THE ORIGINAL NATIVE AMERICANS.

I recollect when I was staying in America, an old Delaware Indian came to Boston to sell some skins and furs, and he called at the house where I was stopping. He had once been a chief among the Indians, but was now poor.

I went to this Indian's home, which was a little hut near Mount Holyoke. We found his wife and his three children; two boys and a girl. They came out to meet us, and were very glad to see their father and me.

I was very hungry and tired when I arrived. The Indian's wife roasted some bear's flesh, and gave us some bread made of pounded corn, for our supper.

I then went to bed on some bear skins, and slept very well. Early in the morning I was called to go hunting with the Indian and his two sons. It was a fine bright morning in October. The sun was shining on the tops of the mountains; we climbed Mount Holyoke, through the woods, and ascended a high rock, from which we could see a beautiful valley far below us, in the centre of which was the little town of Northampton, much smaller than it is now.

"Do you see those houses?" said the Indian to me, "When my grandfather was a boy, there was not a house where you see so many: that valley which now belongs to white men, belonged to red men."

"Then the red men were rich and happy; now they are poor and wretched. Then that beautiful river which you see running through the valley, and which is called the Connecticut, was theirs. They owned these fine mountains too, they hunted in these woods, and fished in that river, and were numerous and powerful,—now they are few and weak."

"But how has this change happened?" said I, "who has taken your lands from you, and made you so miserable?"

"I will tell you all about that to-night," said he, "when we return home."

We proceeded cautiously through the woods, and had not gone far when the Indian beckoned us all to stop. "Look yonder," said he to me, "on that high rock above us!" I did so, but could see nothing. "Look again," said he; I did, and saw a young hind standing upon the point of a rock which hung over the valley; she was a beautiful little animal, full of spirit, with large black eyes, slender legs and of a reddish brown colour.

He now selected a choice arrow, placed it on the bow, and sent it whizzing through the air. It struck directly through the heart. The little animal sprang violently forward, over the rock, and fell dead many feet below, where Whampum's sons soon found it; we now returned to the wigwam, carrying the fawn with us.

In the evening I reminded him of his promise to tell me how the Indians had been robbed of their lands and reduced to poverty. He accordingly began as follows:—

"A great many years ago," said he, "when men with white skins had never been seen in this land, some Indians who were out fishing at a place where the sea widens, espied at a great distance something very large, floating on the water, and such as they had never seen before.

"These Indians immediately returning to the shore, apprized their countrymen of what they had observed, and pressed them to go out with them and discover what it might be. They hurried out together, and saw with astonishment what the others had described, but could not agree upon what it was; some believed it to be an uncommonly large fish or animal, whilst others were of opinion that it must be a very large house floating on the sea.

"They sent off messengers to carry the news to their scattered chiefs and warriors that they should come together immediately.

"The chiefs were soon assembled and deliberating as to the manner in which they should receive the Manitou or Supreme Being on his arrival. Every measure was taken to be well provided with plenty of meat for a sacrifice, the women were desired to prepare the best victuals, all the idols were examined and put in order, and a grand dance was supposed not only to be agreeable to the Great Being, but it was believed that it might tend to appease him if he was angry with them.

"Distracted between hope and fear, they were at a loss what to do; a dance, however, commenced in great confusion; fresh runners arrive, declaring it to be a large house, of various colours, and crowded with living creatures.

"Many are for running off into the woods, but are pressed by others to stay, in order not to give offence to their visitors, who might find them out and destroy them. The house at last stops, and a canoe of small size comes on shore, with a man clothed in red, and some others in it; some stay with his canoe to guard it. The chiefs and wise men assembled in council, form themselves into a large circle, towards which the man in red approaches, with two others; he salutes them with a friendly countenance, and they return the salute in the same manner; they are lost in admiration, the dress, the manner, the whole appearance of the unknown strangers is to them a subject of wonder; but they are particularly struck with him who wore the red coat, all glittering with gold, which they could in no manner account for.

"He surely must be the great Manitou; but why should he have a white skin? Meanwhile a large Hack-hack is brought by one of his servants, from which an unknown liquid is poured out into a small cup, and handed to the supposed Manitou; he drinks,—has the cup filled again, and hands it to the chief standing next to him; the chief receives it, but only smells the contents and passes it on to the next chief, who does the same.

"The glass or cup thus passes through the circle without the liquor being tasted by any one, and is upon the point of being returned to the red-clothed Manitou, when one of the Indians, a brave man and a great warrior, suddenly jumps up and harangues the assembly, on the impropriety of returning the cup with its content: It was handed to them, said he, by the Manitou, that they should drink out of it as he had done: to follow his example would be pleasing to him, but to return what he had given to them, might provoke his wrath, and bring destruction on them; and since the orator believed it for the good of the nation, that the contents should be drunk, and as no one else would do it, he would drink it himself, let the consequences be what they might: it was better for one man to die, than that a whole nation should be destroyed.

"He then took the cup, and bidding the assembly a solemn farewell, at once drank up its whole contents. Every eye was fixed on the resolute chief, to see what effect the unknown liquor would produce.

"He soon began to stagger, and at last fell prostrate on the ground; his companions now bemoan his fate, he falls into a sound sleep, and they think he is dead: he wakes again:—he asks for more, his wish is granted; the whole assembly then imitate him, and all become intoxicated.

"After this general intoxication had ceased, the man with the red clothes, who had remained in his great canoe while it lasted, returned again and distributed presents among them, consisting of beads, axes, shoes and stockings, such as white people wear.

"They soon became familiar with each other, and began to converse by signs; the strangers made them understand that they would not stay here, that they would return home again, but would pay them another visit next year, when they would bring them more presents and stay with them awhile.

"They went away, as they had said, and returned in the following season, when both parties were much rejoiced to see each other; but the white men laughed at the Indians, for they had the axes and hoes, which they had given them the year before, hanging to their breasts, as ornaments, and the stockings were made use of as tobacco pouches. The whites now put handles to the axes for them, and cut down trees before their eyes, hoed up the ground, and put the stockings on their legs: here, they say, a general laughter ensued among the Indians, that they had remained ignorant of the use of such valuable tools, and had borne the weight of them hanging to their necks for such a length of time. They took every white man they saw for an inferior attendant on the supreme Manitou in the red laced clothes.

"As they became daily more familiar with the Indians, the white men proposed to stay with us, and we readily consented.

"It was we who so kindly received them in our country, we took them by the hand and bade them welcome to sit down by our side and live with us as brothers; but how did they requite our kindness? They first asked only for a little land, on which to raise bread for themselves and their families, and pasture for their cattle, which we freely gave them; they soon wanted more, which we also gave them; they saw the game in the woods, which the Great Spirit had given us for our subsistence, and they wanted that too; they penetrated into the woods in quest of game; they discovered spots of land which pleased them, that land they also wanted; and because we were loath to part with it, as we saw they had already more than they had need of, they took it from us by force, and drove us to a great distance from our ancient homes; they looked everywhere for good spots of land, and when they found one, they immediately, and without ceremony, possessed themselves of it; but when at last they came to our favourite spots, those which lay most convenient to our fisheries, then bloody wars ensued. We would have been contented that the white people and we should have lived quietly beside each other, but these white men encroached so fast upon us, that we saw at once we should lose all if we did not resist them. The wars that we carried on against each other were long and cruel,—we were enraged when we saw the white people put our friends and relatives, whom they had taken prisoners, on board their ships, whether to drown or sell them as slaves in the country from which they came, we know not; but certain it is, that none of them have ever returned, or even been heard of.

"At last they got possession of the whole country, which the Great Spirit had given us; one of our tribes was forced to wander far to the north, others dispersed in small bodies, and sought refuge where they could.

"How long we shall be permitted to remain in this asylum, the Great Spirit only knows. The whites will not rest contented till they shall have destroyed the last of us, and made us disappear entirely from the face of the earth."

The old Indian said no more: he looked sad, and his two sons looked sad also; and I shall never forget the impression his story made upon my mind.

Thus, these good Indians, with a kind of melancholy pleasure, recite the long history of their sufferings; and often have I listened to their painful details, until I have felt ashamed of being a white man.

A few days after this we set out upon another hunting excursion, and again climbed the mountains. We had proceeded some distance when we heard the report of a gun, and coming round the point of a rock which lay just before us, we saw a Delaware Indian hunter, who had just discharged his carabine at a huge bear, and broken its backbone; the animal fell, and set up a most plaintive cry; something like that of the panther when he is hungry.

The Indian includes all savage beasts in the number of his enemies, and when he has conquered one, he taunts him before he kills him, in the same strain as he would a conquered enemy of a hostile tribe.

Instead of giving the bear another shot, the hunter stood close to him, and addressed him in these words:—

"Hark ye! bear; you are a coward, and no warrior, as you pretend to be. Were you a warrior, you would show it by your firmness, and would not cry and whimper, like an old woman. You know, bear, that our tribes are at war with each other, and that yours were the aggressors." As you may suppose, I was not a little surprised at the delivery of this curious invective.

CHAPTER XV.

PARLEY TELLS ABOUT THE UNITED STATES.

The English settlements in America grew very rapidly into power and importance. The French settlements also increased in extent and influence, and a rivalry between the French and English, fostered and nourished by the "*natural enmity*" which was said to subsist between the Gauls and the Britons, broke out at last in terrible warfare. War is very frightful under any circumstances. It looks very much like murder; and, even at the best of times, a battle-field reminds us of Cain and Abel. Brother slaughters brother, and the conqueror rejoices and describes his sanguinary work as "a glorious victory." In the war between the English and French settlers in America, a new and atrocious feature was introduced. The Indians were engaged, for pay and powder, on either side, to commit the most hideous cruelties; and things were done which must not be told here, but the very thought of which should make us shudder and turn pale.

The English got the better of the French, and they took Quebec, a strong city in Canada. General Wolfe, a young man and an excellent soldier, captured the city; but it cost him his life. During the heat of the engagement, Wolfe was shot. "Support me," said he to an officer near him; "do not let my brave fellows see my face!" He was removed to the rear, and water was brought to quench his thirst. Just then a cry was heard, "They run! they run!" "Who runs?" exclaimed Wolfe, faintly raising himself. "The enemy!" was the reply. "Then," said he, "I die content," and expired.

The result of the war in which General Wolfe perished, left a vast amount of debt as a heavy weight upon the country. The English settlers had fought very bravely all through the war, and they thought that the English at home ought to pay the debt, and not tax them for its payment. But the king and the parliament thought differently. They taxed the American settlers very heavily; they would listen to no remonstrance; and, when some signs were given of resistance, they were threatened with punishment, like so many unruly schoolboys. Certain privileges which had been granted them were taken away, and troops sent out to enforce obedience. One very objectionable tax to the Americans was a stamp duty on newspapers. Another was a tax on tea. They urged that it was unfair for the British government to tax them without they were allowed to send members to Parliament to look after their interests; but remonstrance only tended to make the British government more determined; and so at last they came to what somebody has called gunpowder law, that is to say, fighting.

I need not enter on the events of the war. It ended in the triumph of the American settlers, and in the declaration of American independence and the formation of the United States. The foremost man, both as a statesman and a soldier, in the conduct of the war, on the part of the Americans, was George Washington. He was elected three times to the presidency, and no name is more revered than his by the Americans.

Since the separation of America from England, more than one quarrel has occurred between them. That which most vitally touches the future prosperity of the states is the warfare which now rages between the northern and southern sections of the republic. Most of you are aware that slavery prevails to a great extent in America. The negroes or blacks (the word *negro* means *black*) are more particularly found in the southern states. The northern states do not *hold* slaves, but they have so far *held* with slavery as to give up runaways, and tolerate the laws which make a man—because he was black—a mere beast of burden. A quarrel, however, on this question, and others of minor importance, has at last broken out between the north and south. The southerners have separated from the northerners, and established a new republic of their own. Their *right* to do this has been denied by the north, and a civil war has commenced in consequence. What may be the final result it is impossible for any one to predict. The quarrel threatened at one time to involve a war with England; but this is no longer apprehended. It seems a very sad thing that a people so clever, so enterprising, so prosperous as the Americans, should, by a quarrel and separation among themselves, endanger—if they do not entirely overthrow—one of the most important states in the world. We cannot forget what it is that lies at the bottom of the mischief—SLAVERY.

> "O execrable crime! so to aspire
> Above our brethren, to ourselves assuming
> Authority usurped from God, not given.
> He gave us only over beast, fish, fowl,
> Dominion absolute; that right we hold
> By his donation: but man over man
> He made not lord—such title to himself
> Reserving, human left from human free."

I may now tell you something about some of the chief cities in the United States.

New York is the principal seaport and commercial metropolis of the States. It is situated at the southern extremity of an island called Manhattan Island, near the mouth of the Hudson river. Its progress has been very rapid, and its population is more than double that of any other city in the new world. The approach to the city is very fine—the shores of the bay being wooded down to the water's edge, and thickly studded with farms, villages, and country seats. New York measures about ten miles round. It is triangular in form. The principal street is Broadway, a spacious thoroughfare extending in a straight line through the centre of the city. The houses have a clean, fresh, cheerful appearance; many of the stores or shops are highly decorated; the public buildings, including the churches, while they can make no pretension to grandeur, are good of their kind; the university is probably the finest building in the city. The hotels in New York are far more extensive than anything of the kind in Europe, and they are fitted up and conducted on a scale of princely grandeur. The city of New York was founded by the Dutch in 1621, and called New Amsterdam; but it was given to the Duke of York (afterwards James II.) in 1604, and was henceforth called by his name. The first congress of the United States was held there in 1789.

Washington is the government capital of the States, and is so called in honour of the distinguished man—the father of the Republic—to whom I have already alluded. The entrance to the city by the Pennsylvanian avenue is 100 feet wide, and planted with some of the trees. The president's residence is called the "White House." The chief public offices and halls for the assembly of congress are contained in one building known as the Capitol. It stands on a hill, and is said to be the finest building in the Union. It is surrounded by ornamental grounds, and overlooks the river Potomac.

BOSTON is a maritime city, and a great place of trade; it is situated on an extensive bay, and is connected with the interior of the country by canals, railways, and river navigation. It is the great seat of the American ice trade. In the history of the war of independence it occupies a conspicuous place, as the Bostonians displayed great energy in asserting popular rights. At Boston, when the "taxed tea" was sent over by the British government, a number of the citizens disguised themselves as Mohawk Indians, boarded the ships in which it had been brought over, seized upon and staved the chests, and threw their contents into the sea. This affair was known as the Boston tea party. Boston is the birth-place of Dr. Benjamin Franklin—the "Poor Richard" of whom I have no doubt you have often heard, and whose excellent advice cannot be too well remembered nor too carefully applied.

CHARLESTON is another of the principal sea-ports of the States. It is the largest town in South Carolina, and is situated at a low point of land at the confluence of two rivers. It is the stronghold of slavery. One of the most recent events connected with it is that of the Northerners blocking up the harbour by sinking several ships, laden with stones, at the entrance. This is a very barbarous act, as it closes—perhaps for ever—one of the first ports in America.

PHILADELPHIA is the last city I shall mention. It is the great Quaker city; its streets are remarkable for their regularity, and the houses and stores for the peculiar air of cleanness which they exhibit. The public buildings are nearly all of white marble. It is distinguished for its vast number of charitable institutions and religious edifices, and it is a thriving place of business. The city was founded by William Penn in 1682. There is a monument marking the site of the signing of Penn's famous treaty with the Indians. With some little account of this treaty I shall conclude my notice of America.

King Charles II. made a grant of land to Penn, but this good man would not enter upon its possession until after he had arranged a treaty with those to whom he justly thought it more fairly belonged than to the King of England—namely, with the Indians. He consequently convened a meeting—under the wide spreading branches of an elm tree, the Indian chiefs assembled. They were unarmed; the old men sat in a half-moon upon the ground, the middle aged in the same figure, at a little distance from them; the younger men formed a third semicircle in the rear. Before them stood William Penn,—a light blue sash, the only mark which distinguished him from his friends, bound round his waist.

"'Thou'lt find,' said the quaker, 'in me and mine,
But friends and brothers to thee and thine,
Who above no power, admit no line,
    Twixt the red man and the white.'

And bright was the spot where the quaker came,
To leave his hat, his drab, and his name,
That will sweetly sound from the trumpet of fame,
   Till its final blast shall die."

It is to be regretted that the speeches of the Indians on this memorable day have not come down to us. It is only known that they solemnly pledged themselves to live with William Penn and his people in peace and amity so long as the sun and moon should endure. This was the only treaty, it has been said, between these people and the Christians that was *not* ratified by an oath, and that was *never* broken.

AUSTRALIA.

CHAPTER XVI.

PARLEY TELLS ABOUT NEW SOUTH WALES.

At the termination of the American war, of which I have just given you a short account, the United States of America, which had been called by England her American Colonies, ceased to be any longer subject to Great Britain.

The province of Virginia, in America, had for a long time been the only authorized outlet for those criminals in Great Britain and Ireland, who had been sentenced to transportation.

It now became necessary for the English government to fix upon some other country, to which those of her subjects might be transported, who were condemned to banishment for their crimes.

After much deliberation in the British Parliament, it was determined to form a penal settlement in New South Wales.

If you will look at a globe, or, if you have not a globe, at a map of the world, turning the South Pole from you, or uppermost, and, supposing yourself to be in a ship, sail across the

Atlantic Ocean till you come to the Equator, which is an imaginary line that divides the northern half of the globe from the southern; then "cross the line," as it is called, and sail along the South Atlantic, in the direction of the coast of South America, till you arrive at its southern extremity, which you will see is called Cape Horn; then sailing round Cape Horn, (which is called doubling Cape Horn), and directing your course westward, right across the Great Pacific Ocean. After having sailed across these three great oceans, you will find yourself, if you have a prosperous voyage, exactly on the opposite side of the globe, and before you, an extensive chain of large islands, lying off the South-eastern extremity of the continent of Asia.

This group of islands has been named Australasia, which means Southern Asia, and the largest of these, which is the largest island in the whole world, has been called Australia, or New Holland.

This is so large an island, that if you were to divide the whole of Europe into ten parts, New Holland is as large as nine of them: and hence, from its great extent, some geographers have dignified it with the title of a continent.

The northern and western coasts of this vast island were discovered by a succession of Dutch navigators, who gave them the name of New Holland.

The eastern coast, which has been explored, and taken possession of by the English, was discovered by Capt. Cook, who gave it the name of New South Wales.

At the southern extremity of Australia or New Holland, you will see VAN DIEMEN'S LAND, which was discovered by Tasman, one of the Dutch navigators, who was sent from Batavia by Anthony Van Diemen, the Dutch governor-general of the Indies, to survey the coast of New Holland.

In this voyage Tasman discovered an extensive country lying to the south of New Holland; in giving a name to which, he immortalized his patron, by calling it "Van Diemen's Land," having no suspicion at the time that it was an island.

It was not till the year 1798 that it was discovered to be such; as in all the old maps and charts it is represented as part of the main land of New Holland.

This important discovery was effected in an open boat, by Mr. Bass, a surgeon in the royal navy, who found it to be separated from Australia by a broad strait, which has ever since borne the name of its discoverer, "BASS' STRAITS."

A fleet of eleven sail was assembled at Portsmouth in March, 1783, for the formation of the proposed settlement on the coast of New Holland.

On board of these vessels were embarked 600 male, and 250 female convicts, with a guard consisting of about 200 soldiers, with their proper officers. Forty women, wives of the marines, were also permitted to accompany their husbands, together with their children.

Captain Arthur Phillip, an officer highly qualified in every respect for the arduous undertaking, was appointed governor of the proposed colony.

The little fleet which was thus placed under the command of Captain Phillip, and which has ever since been designated by the colonists *"the first fleet,"* set sail from Portsmouth on the 13th of May 1787, and arrived at Botany Bay, in New South Wales, in January 1788, after a long, but comparatively prosperous voyage of eight months and upwards.

Captain Phillip soon found, to his disappointment, that Botany Bay was by no means an eligible harbour; nor was it, in other respects, suitable for the establishment of a colony, and he determined, even before any number of the convicts had been permitted to land, to search for a more eligible site.

In Captain Cook's chart of the coast, another opening had been laid down, a few miles to the northward of Botany Bay, on the authority of a seaman of the name of Jackson, who had seen it from the foretop-mast-head; and Captain Cook, conceiving it to be nothing more than a harbour for boats, which it was not worth his while to examine, called it Port Jackson.

It is no wonder that Captain Cook came to this conclusion; for no opening of any kind can be perceived till you come close in with the land.

This opening Captain Phillip examined, and the result of that examination was the splendid discovery of Port Jackson,—one of the finest harbours, whether for extent or security, in the world.

To this harbour the fleet was immediately removed, and the settlement was ultimately formed at the head of Sydney Cove, one of the numerous and romantic inlets of Port Jackson.

The labour and patience required, and the difficulties which the first settlers must have had to encounter, are incalculable; but their success has been complete.

The forest has been cleared away, the corn-field and the orchard have supplanted the wild grass and the bush, and towns and villages have arisen as if by magic. You may hear the lowing of herds where, a few years before, you would have trembled at the wild whoop of the savage, and the stillness of that once solitary shore is broken by the sound of wheels and the busy hum of commerce.

CHAPTER XVII.

PARLEY DESCRIBES THE INHABITANTS, VEGETABLES, AND ANIMALS OF AUSTRALIA—THE BRITISH SETTLEMENTS—THE GOLD REGIONS—RECENT EXPLORATIONS

The natives of this part of Australia are, beyond comparison, the most barbarous on the surface of the globe.

They are hideously ugly, with flat noses, wide nostrils, eyes sunk in the head, and overshadowed with thick eyebrows. The mouth very wide, lips thick and prominent, hair black, but not woolly; the colour of the skin varies from dark bronze to jet black. Their stature is below the middle size, and they are remarkably thin and ill-made.

To add to their natural deformity, they thrust a bone through the cartilage of the nose, and stick with gum to their hair matted moss, the teeth of men, sharks, and kangaroos, the tails of dogs, and jaw-bones of fish.

On particular occasions they ornament themselves with red and white clay, using the former when preparing to fight, and the latter for the more peaceful amusement of dancing. The fashion of these ornaments was left to each person's taste, and some, when decorated in their best manner, looked perfectly horrible: nothing could appear more terrible than a black and dismal face, with a large white circle drawn round each eye.

They scarify the skin in every part with sharp shells.

The women and female children are generally found to want the first two joints of the little finger of the left hand, which are taken off while they are infants, and the reason they assign is, that they would be in the way in winding the fish-lines over the hand.

The men all want one of their front teeth, which is knocked out when they arrive at the age of fifteen or sixteen, with many ridiculous ceremonies; but the boys are not allowed to consider themselves as men before they have undergone that operation.

They live chiefly on fish, which they sometimes spear and sometimes net; the women, on the parts of the coast, aiding to catch them with the hook and line.

"The facility," (observes Captain Sturt), "with which they procured fish was really surprising.

"They would slip, feet foremost, into the water, as they walked along the bank of the river, as if they had accidentally done so; but, in reality, to avoid the splash they would have made if they had plunged in head foremost.

"As surely as a native disappeared under the surface of the water, so surely would he re-appear, with a fish writhing upon the point of his short spear.

"The very otter scarcely exceeds them in power over the finny race, and so true is the aim of these savages, even under the water, that all the fish we procured from them were pierced either close behind the lateral fin or in the very centre of the head."

If a dead whale happens to be cast on the shore, numbers flock to it, from every part of the coast, and they feast sumptuously while any part remains.

Those in the interior are stated to live on grubs, insects, ants and their eggs, kangaroos, when they can catch them, fern roots, various kinds of berries, and honey; caterpillars and worms also form part of their food.

Captain Phillip took every possible pains to reclaim these ignorant savages, and he once nearly lost his life in endeavouring to conciliate a party of them, having ventured amongst them unarmed for that purpose; one of the savages threw a spear which pierced the upper part of his shoulder and came out at his back.

But all the efforts of the governor to effect the permanent civilization of these miserable people proved utterly abortive.

They possess the faculty of mimickry or imitation to a very considerable degree. I was walking with a friend, one beautiful evening, on the banks of the Paramatta, when Bungarry, chief of the Sydney tribe of black natives, was pulling down the river with his two jins, or wives, in a boat which he had received as a present from the governor. My friend accosted him on his coming up with us, and the good-natured chief immediately desired his *jins* to rest upon their oars, for he was rowed by his wives. During the short conversation that ensued, my friend requested Bungarry to show how governor Macquarrie made a bow.

Bungarry happened to be dressed in the old uniform of a military officer, and standing up in the stern of his boat, and taking off his cocked hat, with the requisite punctilio, he made a low formal bow, with all the dignity and grace of a general officer of the old school.

The rich variety of vegetation on the Illawarra mountain, which is a lofty range running parallel with the coast, contrasts beautifully with the richness of the scenery. The fern tree, shooting up its rough stem, about the thickness of a small boat's mast, to the height of fifteen or twenty feet, and then, all at once shooting out a number of leaves in every direction, each at four or five feet in length, and exactly similar in appearance to the leaf of the common fern; while palms of various botanical species, are ever and anon shooting up their tall slender branchless stems to the height of seventy or a hundred feet, and then forming a large canopy of leaves, each of which bends gracefully outwards and then downwards, like a Prince of Wales' feathers.

Another beautiful species met with in the low grounds of Illawarra, is the fan palm, or cabbage tree, and another equally graceful in its outline, is called by the natives Bangalo.

The nettle tree, which is also met with in the bushes, is not only seen by the traveller, but occasionally felt, and remembered, for its name is highly descriptive.

Both the animal and vegetable creation in Australia, are wholly different from those in every other part of the world.

To show that the existence of a thing was not believed in, it was compared to a *black swan*, but in New Holland we find black swans, and blue frogs; red lobsters, and blue crabs; flying opossums, and beasts with bills like ducks; fish that hop about on dry land, and quadrupeds that lay eggs.

The quadrupeds hitherto discovered, with very few exceptions, are all of the kangaroo or opossum tribe; having their hinder legs long, out of all proportion when compared with the length of the fore legs, and a sack under the belly of the female for the reception of the young.

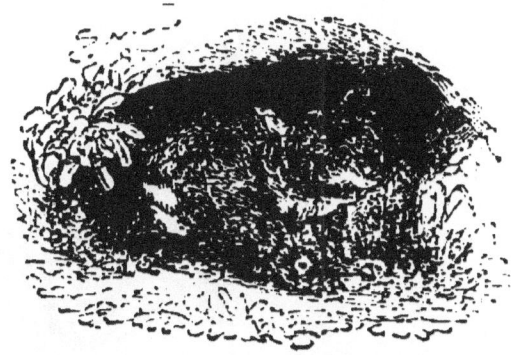

They have kangaroo rats, and dogs of the jackal kind, all exactly alike; and a little animal of the bear tribe, named the wombat, but the largest quadruped at present discovered is the kangaroo.

These pretty nearly complete the catalogue of four-footed animals yet known on this vast island.

There is, however, an animal which resembles nothing in the creation but itself, and which neither belongs to beast, bird or fish.

This animal is called the Duck-billed Platypus.

Of all the quadrupeds yet known, this seems the most extraordinary in its conformation; exhibiting the perfect semblance of the beak of a duck on the head of a quadruped.

The head is flattish, and rather small than large; the mouth or snout so exactly resembles that of some broad-billed species of duck, that it might be mistaken for one.

The birds and fish are no less singular than the beasts. There is a singular fish, which when left uncovered by the ebbing of the tide, leaps about like the grasshopper, by means of strong fins.

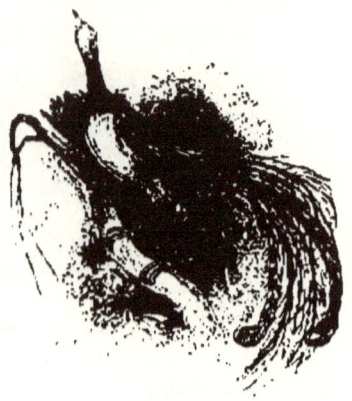

The Mœnura Superba, with its scalloped tail feathers, is perhaps the most singular and beautiful of that elegant race of bird, known by the name of Birds of Paradise.

Cockatoos, Parrots, and Parroquets, are innumerable, and of great variety.

The Nonpareil Parrot is perhaps the most beautiful bird of the parrot tribe in the whole world.

The Mountain Eagle is a magnificent creature; but the Emu, or New Holland Cassowary, is perhaps the tallest and loftiest bird that exists.

The capital of the colony, and the seat of the colonial Government is Sydney. The Town of Sydney is beautifully situated in Sydney Cove, which I told you is one of the romantic inlets of Port Jackson, about seven miles from the entrance of the harbour. The headlands at the mouth of the harbour form one of the grandest features in the natural scenery of the country.

It is not, however, a distant or cursory glance that will give you a just idea of the importance of this busy capital.

In order to form a just estimation of it, you should take a boat and proceed from Sydney Cove to Darling Harbour, you will then see the whole extent of the eastern shore of the latter capacious basin equally crowded with warehouses, stores, dock-yards, mills, and wharfs; the store-houses built on the most magnificent scale, and with the best and most substantial materials. The population of Sydney is supposed now to exceed 10,000 persons.

The second town in the colony is Paramatta. It is distant about fourteen miles from Sydney, being pleasantly situated at the head of one of the navigable arms of Port Jackson. It contains nearly 5,000 inhabitants. The other towns in the colony, are Windsor, Liverpool, Campbell Town, Newcastle and Maitland. The last will doubtless ere long be the second in the colony, as it is situated at the head of the navigation of Hunter's river.

Very fine roads have been formed in Australia, particularly one leading across the Blue mountains to Bathurst, on the western side of that range, which is 180 miles from Sydney.

The openness of the country around Bathurst is more favourable for hunting and shooting than most other parts of the colony.

The Kangaroo and the Emu are both hunted with dogs; they are both feeble animals, but they are not altogether destitute of the means of defence.

In addition to swiftness of foot, the Emu has a great muscular power in his long iron limbs, and can give an awkward blow to his pursuer, by striking out at him behind, like a young horse, while the Kangaroo, when brought to bay by the dogs, rests himself on his strong muscular tail, seizes the dog with his little hands or fore-feet, and thrusts at him with one of his hind feet, which is armed for that purpose with a single sharp-pointed hoof, and perhaps lay his side completely open.

When hotly pursued, the kangaroo sometimes takes to the water, where, if he happen to be followed by a dog, he has a singular advantage over all other quadrupeds of his own size, from his being able to stand erect in pretty deep water.

In this position he waits for the dog, and when the latter comes close up to him, he seizes him with his fore-feet and presses him under water till he is drowned.

The Bustard, or native turkey, is occasionally shot in the Bathurst country. It sometimes weighs eighteen pounds, and is different from the common turkey, in the flesh of the legs being white, while that of the breast is dark-coloured.

Among the natives the old men have alone the privilege of eating the Emu, and married people only are permitted to eat ducks.

The natives suffer no animal, however small, to escape them.

One of the blacks being anxious to get an Opossum out of a dead tree, every branch of which was hollow, asked for a tomahawk, with which he cut a hole in the trunk above where he thought the animal lay concealed. He found, however, that he had cut too low, and that it had run higher up. This made it necessary to smoke it out; he accordingly got some dry grass, and having set fire to it, stuffed it into the hole he had cut.

A raging fire soon kindled in the tree, where the current of air was great, and dense columns of smoke issued from the end of each branch as thick as that from the chimney of a steam-engine.

The shell of the tree was so thin, that I thought it would soon be burnt through, and that the tree would fall; but the black had no such fears, and, ascending to the highest branch, he waited anxiously for the poor little wretch he had thus surrounded with dangers, and devoted to destruction; and no sooner did it appear half singed and half roasted, than he seized upon it and threw it down to us with an air of triumph. The effect of the scene, in so lonely a forest, was very fine. The roaring of the fire in the tree, the fearless attitude of the savage, and the associations which his colour and appearance called up, enveloped as he was in smoke, were singular, and still dwell in my recollection. He had not long left the tree, when it fell with a tremendous crash, and was, when we next passed that way, a mere heap of ashes.

The territory of the colony has been divided into ten counties, named as follows:—Cumberland, Camden, Argyll, Westmoreland, Londonderry, Boxburgh, Northumberland, Durham, Ayr, and Cambridge.

I will now give you a short account of Van Diemen's Land.

This fair and fertile island lies, as I have told you, at the southern extremity of New Holland, from which it is separated by Bass' Straits.

Its medial length from north to south is about 185 miles, and its breadth from east to west is 166 miles.

Its surface possesses every variety of mountain, hill, and dale; of forests and open meadows; of inland lakes, rivers and inlets of the sea, forming safe and commodious harbours; and every natural requisite that can render a country valuable or agreeable.

It enjoys a temperate climate, which is perhaps not very different from that of England, though less subject to violent changes.

The island is intersected by two fine rivers, rising near the centre; the one named the Tamar, falling into Bass' Straits, on the north, and forming Port Dalrymple; the other the Derwent, which discharges itself into the sea, on the south-eastern extremity. Hobart Town, the capital, is situated on the right bank of the Derwent, about five miles from the sea.

The natives of Van Diemen's Land are described by all the navigators, as a mild, affable, good-humoured and inoffensive race.

Though they are obviously the same race of people as those of New Holland, and go entirely naked, both men and women, yet their language is altogether different.

The British settlements in Australia are both numerous and important. The oldest, most extensive, and valuable, was founded, as we have shewn already, at Sydney. The island of Tasmania was next occupied; within the last few years we have established the colonies of Port Phillip, Melbourne, Victoria, Cooksland, and others. The progress of these settlements has been rapid.

An extraordinary increase to emigration to Australia was given by the discovery of the Gold Regions.

For many years reports had been current that the Australian Alps and the Snowy Mountains were full of gold, but it was not till after the Californian discoveries that any was found in Australia.

Two shepherds were the first persons who found any gold, and for a long time they successfully concealed the source from which they obtained it; but being watched, their secret was discovered, and the news spread like wild-fire over the colony. Everybody was mad to go gold hunting; shepherds forsook their flocks; traders closed their stores; sailors ran away from their ships; servants threw up their situations; everybody was mad to visit this newly-discovered Tom Tiddler's ground, to pick up gold and silver. A groom informed his master, in one instance, that he would stop with him, as he had been in the family for five years, for a guinea a day, if it would be any convenience to him. Another family was left with only a boy of sixteen to attend them, and his stipulations were—two pounds a week, and wine to his dinner! In one year the population of Melbourne rose from 23,000 to 85,000 inhabitants; the town of Geelong trebled its numbers; perhaps never in the whole history of the world had there been so extraordinary an emigration.

As a monument of the golden wealth of Australia, there is in the International Exhibition a wooden obelisk dead gilt on the outside. This column is nearly seventy feet high, and some ten feet square at the base. It represents exactly the bulk of gold which Australia has sent to this country since 1851, and which in all amounts to nearly 800 tons. Valuing the precious metal at its ascertainable worth, it appears that gold to the value of upwards of £15,000 sterling was dug from the bowels of the earth, washed from the sand of the rivers, or discovered by fortunate diggers in various parts of Australia in a single year.

The interior of Australia is still comparatively unknown. Last year an expedition was undertaken to discover a way across the Continent, and entrusted to a vigilant and enterprising commander named Burke. Although a certain amount of success attended the object of the expedition, the fate of Burke and his immediate companions was most deplorable. They perished by starvation!

CONCLUSION.

I have now told you all that my present limits will admit, of those interesting portions of the globe, called America and Australia, and I wish you to read again all that I have said, and I wish you also to view the inhuman conduct of the first discoverers of the former with proper feelings of aversion. If you have read an account of William Penn's first colony of Pennsylvania, you will see that his was the only just way of establishing himself among the Indians. You must rejoice within yourselves on this occasion, that they were not Englishmen who practised these acts of cruelty and treachery towards the unoffending Mexicans and Peruvians. The workings of Providence are full of mystery, and I cannot help thinking that the state of anarchy and civil war in which Spain and Portugal are now and ever have been engaged, is an act of retribution awarded to their barbarity in the great scheme of God's providence.

It makes one blush for the sake of Christianity, to think that the perpetrators of the outrages upon the original possessors of the Americas were persons professing that sublime religion, —and that in the midst of their slaughter and plunder, they impiously held forth the cross of Christ. The confiding but dignified nature of the idolatrous Mexicans, did much more honour to the purity of the Christian religion than did the base treachery of their invaders, who professed Christ but knew him not.

Had they by mildness, perseverance, and reason convinced the inhabitants of the truth of the Christian religion, they might have become faithful converts, but it was unreasonable to expect that they should cast off the religion which their forefathers had professed, for a religion which they knew not at all, and the professors of which came with the sword to deprive them of their lives and their property.

I wish you, my young friends, to weigh all these circumstances whenever you read. It will impress the different subjects more thoroughly upon your memory; and if your minds be properly constituted, it will cultivate the good and eradicate the bad. I will again ask you to read this book a second time, and refer occasionally to the maps. And now good-bye!

THE END.

BILLING, PRINTER AND STEREOTYPER, GUILDFORD, SURREY.

END OF THE PROJECT GUTENBERG EBOOK PETER PARLEY'S TALES ABOUT AMERICA AND AUSTRALIA

******* This file should be named 16891-h.txt or 16891-h.zip *******

This and all associated files of various formats will be found in:
http://www.gutenberg.org/1/6/8/9/16891

Updated editions will replace the previous one--the old editions will be renamed.

Creating the works from public domain print editions means that no one owns a United States copyright in these works, so the Foundation (and you!) can copy and distribute it in the United States without permission and without paying copyright royalties. Special rules, set forth in the General Terms of Use part of this license, apply to copying and distributing Project Gutenberg-tm electronic works to protect the PROJECT GUTENBERG-tm concept and trademark. Project Gutenberg is a registered trademark, and may not be used if you charge for the eBooks, unless you receive specific permission. If you do not charge anything for copies of this eBook, complying with the rules is very easy. You may use this eBook for nearly any purpose such as creation of derivative works, reports, performances and research. They may be modified and printed and given away--you may do practically ANYTHING with public domain eBooks. Redistribution is subject to the trademark license, especially commercial redistribution.

```
*** START: FULL LICENSE ***

THE FULL PROJECT GUTENBERG LICENSE
PLEASE READ THIS BEFORE YOU DISTRIBUTE OR USE THIS WORK

To protect the Project Gutenberg-tm mission of promoting the free
distribution of electronic works, by using or distributing this work
(or any other work associated in any way with the phrase "Project
Gutenberg"), you agree to comply with all the terms of the Full Project
Gutenberg-tm License (available with this file or online at
http://gutenberg.org/license).


Section 1.  General Terms of Use and Redistributing Project Gutenberg-tm
electronic works

1.A.  By reading or using any part of this Project Gutenberg-tm
electronic work, you indicate that you have read, understand, agree to
and accept all the terms of this license and intellectual property
(trademark/copyright) agreement.  If you do not agree to abide by all
the terms of this agreement, you must cease using and return or destroy
all copies of Project Gutenberg-tm electronic works in your possession.
If you paid a fee for obtaining a copy of or access to a Project
```

Gutenberg-tm electronic work and you do not agree to be bound by the
terms of this agreement, you may obtain a refund from the person or
entity to whom you paid the fee as set forth in paragraph 1.E.8.

1.B. "Project Gutenberg" is a registered trademark. It may only be
used on or associated in any way with an electronic work by people who
agree to be bound by the terms of this agreement. There are a few
things that you can do with most Project Gutenberg-tm electronic works
even without complying with the full terms of this agreement. See
paragraph 1.C below. There are a lot of things you can do with Project
Gutenberg-tm electronic works if you follow the terms of this agreement
and help preserve free future access to Project Gutenberg-tm electronic
works. See paragraph 1.E below.

1.C. The Project Gutenberg Literary Archive Foundation ("the Foundation"
or PGLAF), owns a compilation copyright in the collection of Project
Gutenberg-tm electronic works. Nearly all the individual works in the
collection are in the public domain in the United States. If an
individual work is in the public domain in the United States and you are
located in the United States, we do not claim a right to prevent you from
copying, distributing, performing, displaying or creating derivative
works based on the work as long as all references to Project Gutenberg
are removed. Of course, we hope that you will support the Project
Gutenberg-tm mission of promoting free access to electronic works by
freely sharing Project Gutenberg-tm works in compliance with the terms of
this agreement for keeping the Project Gutenberg-tm name associated with
the work. You can easily comply with the terms of this agreement by
keeping this work in the same format with its attached full Project
Gutenberg-tm License when you share it without charge with others.

1.D. The copyright laws of the place where you are located also govern
what you can do with this work. Copyright laws in most countries are in
a constant state of change. If you are outside the United States, check
the laws of your country in addition to the terms of this agreement
before downloading, copying, displaying, performing, distributing or
creating derivative works based on this work or any other Project
Gutenberg-tm work. The Foundation makes no representations concerning
the copyright status of any work in any country outside the United
States.

1.E. Unless you have removed all references to Project Gutenberg:

1.E.1. The following sentence, with active links to, or other immediate
access to, the full Project Gutenberg-tm License must appear prominently
whenever any copy of a Project Gutenberg-tm work (any work on which the
phrase "Project Gutenberg" appears, or with which the phrase "Project
Gutenberg" is associated) is accessed, displayed, performed, viewed,
copied or distributed:

This eBook is for the use of anyone anywhere at no cost and with
almost no restrictions whatsoever. You may copy it, give it away or
re-use it under the terms of the Project Gutenberg License included
with this eBook or online at www.gutenberg.org

1.E.2. If an individual Project Gutenberg-tm electronic work is derived
from the public domain (does not contain a notice indicating that it is
posted with permission of the copyright holder), the work can be copied
and distributed to anyone in the United States without paying any fees
or charges. If you are redistributing or providing access to a work
with the phrase "Project Gutenberg" associated with or appearing on the
work, you must comply either with the requirements of paragraphs 1.E.1

- You provide, in accordance with paragraph 1.F.3, a full refund of any
  money paid for a work or a replacement copy, if a defect in the
  electronic work is discovered and reported to you within 90 days
  of receipt of the work.

- You comply with all other terms of this agreement for free
  distribution of Project Gutenberg-tm works.

1.E.9. If you wish to charge a fee or distribute a Project Gutenberg-tm
electronic work or group of works on different terms than are set
forth in this agreement, you must obtain permission in writing from
both the Project Gutenberg Literary Archive Foundation and Michael
Hart, the owner of the Project Gutenberg-tm trademark. Contact the
Foundation as set forth in Section 3 below.

1.F.

1.F.1. Project Gutenberg volunteers and employees expend considerable
effort to identify, do copyright research on, transcribe and proofread
public domain works in creating the Project Gutenberg-tm
collection. Despite these efforts, Project Gutenberg-tm electronic
works, and the medium on which they may be stored, may contain
"Defects," such as, but not limited to, incomplete, inaccurate or
corrupt data, transcription errors, a copyright or other intellectual
property infringement, a defective or damaged disk or other medium, a
computer virus, or computer codes that damage or cannot be read by
your equipment.

1.F.2. LIMITED WARRANTY, DISCLAIMER OF DAMAGES - Except for the "Right
of Replacement or Refund" described in paragraph 1.F.3, the Project
Gutenberg Literary Archive Foundation, the owner of the Project
Gutenberg-tm trademark, and any other party distributing a Project
Gutenberg-tm electronic work under this agreement, disclaim all
liability to you for damages, costs and expenses, including legal
fees. YOU AGREE THAT YOU HAVE NO REMEDIES FOR NEGLIGENCE, STRICT
LIABILITY, BREACH OF WARRANTY OR BREACH OF CONTRACT EXCEPT THOSE
PROVIDED IN PARAGRAPH F3. YOU AGREE THAT THE FOUNDATION, THE
TRADEMARK OWNER, AND ANY DISTRIBUTOR UNDER THIS AGREEMENT WILL NOT BE
LIABLE TO YOU FOR ACTUAL, DIRECT, INDIRECT, CONSEQUENTIAL, PUNITIVE OR
INCIDENTAL DAMAGES EVEN IF YOU GIVE NOTICE OF THE POSSIBILITY OF SUCH
DAMAGE.

1.F.3. LIMITED RIGHT OF REPLACEMENT OR REFUND - If you discover a
defect in this electronic work within 90 days of receiving it, you can
receive a refund of the money (if any) you paid for it by sending a
written explanation to the person you received the work from. If you
received the work on a physical medium, you must return the medium with
your written explanation. The person or entity that provided you with
the defective work may elect to provide a replacement copy in lieu of a
refund. If you received the work electronically, the person or entity
providing it to you may choose to give you a second opportunity to
receive the work electronically in lieu of a refund. If the second copy
is also defective, you may demand a refund in writing without further
opportunities to fix the problem.

1.F.4. Except for the limited right of replacement or refund set forth
in paragraph 1.F.3, this work is provided to you 'AS-IS,' WITH NO OTHER
WARRANTIES OF ANY KIND, EXPRESS OR IMPLIED, INCLUDING BUT NOT LIMITED TO
WARRANTIES OF MERCHANTIBILITY OR FITNESS FOR ANY PURPOSE.

1.F.5. Some states do not allow disclaimers of certain implied
warranties or the exclusion or limitation of certain types of damages.
If any disclaimer or limitation set forth in this agreement violates the
law of the state applicable to this agreement, the agreement shall be
interpreted to make the maximum disclaimer or limitation permitted by
the applicable state law. The invalidity or unenforceability of any
provision of this agreement shall not void the remaining provisions.

1.F.6. INDEMNITY - You agree to indemnify and hold the Foundation, the
trademark owner, any agent or employee of the Foundation, anyone
providing copies of Project Gutenberg-tm electronic works in accordance
with this agreement, and any volunteers associated with the production,
promotion and distribution of Project Gutenberg-tm electronic works,
harmless from all liability, costs and expenses, including legal fees,
that arise directly or indirectly from any of the following which you do
or cause to occur: (a) distribution of this or any Project Gutenberg-tm
work, (b) alteration, modification, or additions or deletions to any
Project Gutenberg-tm work, and (c) any Defect you cause.

Section 2. Information about the Mission of Project Gutenberg-tm

Project Gutenberg-tm is synonymous with the free distribution of
electronic works in formats readable by the widest variety of computers
including obsolete, old, middle-aged and new computers. It exists
because of the efforts of hundreds of volunteers and donations from
people in all walks of life.

Volunteers and financial support to provide volunteers with the
assistance they need, is critical to reaching Project Gutenberg-tm's
goals and ensuring that the Project Gutenberg-tm collection will
remain freely available for generations to come. In 2001, the Project
Gutenberg Literary Archive Foundation was created to provide a secure
and permanent future for Project Gutenberg-tm and future generations.
To learn more about the Project Gutenberg Literary Archive Foundation
and how your efforts and donations can help, see Sections 3 and 4
and the Foundation web page at http://www.gutenberg.org/fundraising/pglaf.

Section 3. Information about the Project Gutenberg Literary Archive
Foundation

The Project Gutenberg Literary Archive Foundation is a non profit
501(c)(3) educational corporation organized under the laws of the
state of Mississippi and granted tax exempt status by the Internal
Revenue Service. The Foundation's EIN or federal tax identification
number is 64-6221541. Contributions to the Project Gutenberg
Literary Archive Foundation are tax deductible to the full extent
permitted by U.S. federal laws and your state's laws.

The Foundation's principal office is located at 4557 Melan Dr. S.
Fairbanks, AK, 99712., but its volunteers and employees are scattered
throughout numerous locations. Its business office is located at
809 North 1500 West, Salt Lake City, UT 84116, (801) 596-1887, email
business@pglaf.org. Email contact links and up to date contact
information can be found at the Foundation's web site and official
page at http://www.gutenberg.org/about/contact

For additional contact information:
     Dr. Gregory B. Newby
     Chief Executive and Director

gbnewby@pglaf.org

Section 4. Information about Donations to the Project Gutenberg
Literary Archive Foundation

Project Gutenberg-tm depends upon and cannot survive without wide
spread public support and donations to carry out its mission of
increasing the number of public domain and licensed works that can be
freely distributed in machine readable form accessible by the widest
array of equipment including outdated equipment. Many small donations
($1 to $5,000) are particularly important to maintaining tax exempt
status with the IRS.

The Foundation is committed to complying with the laws regulating
charities and charitable donations in all 50 states of the United
States. Compliance requirements are not uniform and it takes a
considerable effort, much paperwork and many fees to meet and keep up
with these requirements. We do not solicit donations in locations
where we have not received written confirmation of compliance. To
SEND DONATIONS or determine the status of compliance for any
particular state visit http://www.gutenberg.org/fundraising/pglaf

While we cannot and do not solicit contributions from states where we
have not met the solicitation requirements, we know of no prohibition
against accepting unsolicited donations from donors in such states who
approach us with offers to donate.

International donations are gratefully accepted, but we cannot make
any statements concerning tax treatment of donations received from
outside the United States. U.S. laws alone swamp our small staff.

Please check the Project Gutenberg Web pages for current donation
methods and addresses. Donations are accepted in a number of other
ways including including checks, online payments and credit card
donations. To donate, please visit:
http://www.gutenberg.org/fundraising/donate

Section 5. General Information About Project Gutenberg-tm electronic
works.

Professor Michael S. Hart is the originator of the Project Gutenberg-tm
concept of a library of electronic works that could be freely shared
with anyone. For thirty years, he produced and distributed Project
Gutenberg-tm eBooks with only a loose network of volunteer support.

Project Gutenberg-tm eBooks are often created from several printed
editions, all of which are confirmed as Public Domain in the U.S.
unless a copyright notice is included. Thus, we do not necessarily
keep eBooks in compliance with any particular paper edition.

Each eBook is in a subdirectory of the same number as the eBook's
eBook number, often in several formats including plain vanilla ASCII,
compressed (zipped), HTML and others.

Corrected EDITIONS of our eBooks replace the old file and take over
the old filename and etext number. The replaced older file is renamed.
VERSIONS based on separate sources are treated as new eBooks receiving
new filenames and etext numbers.

Most people start at our Web site which has the main PG search facility:

http://www.gutenberg.org

This Web site includes information about Project Gutenberg-tm,
including how to make donations to the Project Gutenberg Literary
Archive Foundation, how to help produce our new eBooks, and how to
subscribe to our email newsletter to hear about new eBooks.

EBooks posted prior to November 2003, with eBook numbers BELOW #10000,
are filed in directories based on their release date. If you want to
download any of these eBooks directly, rather than using the regular
search system you may utilize the following addresses and just
download by the etext year.

http://www.gutenberg.org/dirs/etext06/

    (Or /etext 05, 04, 03, 02, 01, 00, 99,
     98, 97, 96, 95, 94, 93, 92, 92, 91 or 90)

EBooks posted since November 2003, with etext numbers OVER #10000, are
filed in a different way. The year of a release date is no longer part
of the directory path. The path is based on the etext number (which is
identical to the filename). The path to the file is made up of single
digits corresponding to all but the last digit in the filename. For
example an eBook of filename 10234 would be found at:

http://www.gutenberg.org/dirs/1/0/2/3/10234

or filename 24689 would be found at:
http://www.gutenberg.org/dirs/2/4/6/8/24689

An alternative method of locating eBooks:
http://www.gutenberg.org/dirs/GUTINDEX.ALL

*** END: FULL LICENSE ***

www.ingramcontent.com/pod-product-compliance
Lightning Source LLC
Chambersburg PA
CBHW022012050726
47499CB00007BA/2555